Before Arabella realized what he was about, he took her in his arms and kissed her long and hard. So stunned was she by his sudden maneuver that she did not immediately try to break from his embrace. By the time she had recollected herself, his kiss had stirred in her something quite unlike anything she had ever before experienced. It seemed to sap both her strength and her will, making her a voluntary prisoner to his. . . .

Another Fawcett Book
by Marlene Suson:

THE RELUCTANT HEIRESS

AN
INFAMOUS
BARGAIN

Marlene Suson

FAWCETT CREST • NEW YORK

A Fawcett Crest Book
Published by Ballantine Books
Copyright © 1986 by Marlene Suson

Library of Congress Catalog Card Number: 86-91078

ISBN: 0-449-20929-6

Manufactured in the United States of America

First Edition: May 1986

Chapter 1

A trio of venerable dowagers, irreverently known as the "three harpies" for their devotion to scandalous gossip, watched Arabella Vaughn enter Lady Pyne's ornate London ballroom. Instantly the harpies, who were seated on a yellow damask banquette that commanded an excellent view of the ballroom, took up one of the season's choicest speculations: Would the elusive Lord Estes Howard, son and heir of the dying earl of Woodthorpe, offer for Arabella?

The rumor was particularly tantalizing because young Lord Estes had heretofore never nibbled at any of the lures cast by numerous young ladies of quality. So why would he now choose Arabella Vaughn, who had not even dangled after him? Especially when she was not as beautiful as her younger sister, Beth, a dazzling creature who left the males of the species groping for both quizzing glasses and words adequate to describe such sublimity. Not that Arabella wasn't lovely, but as Lord Alvanley had quipped, it was a case of Venus obscured by the sun.

Of course, Beth was said to be madly in love with young Lieutenant Justin Keats, but such a match would never suit. Although Keats was of excellent family, he was poor as a church mouse, and Beth would have no dowry. Her father was deep in dun territory as a result of the extravagances of his ill-bred second wife. Furthermore, that greedy lady would certainly insist upon a more advantageous marriage than Keats for such a breathtaking beauty as her stepdaughter.

Although Arabella was not as lovely as her sister and had no fortune, even the exacting harpies had to concede that she would still make Lord Estes, who would soon inherit his dying father's vast estates, an excellent match.

A man with Lord Estes's great expectations could afford a portionless bride when her pedigree was as illustrious as Arabella's. Her maternal grandfather had been the twelfth duke of Lysted and her maternal aunt was the formidable duchess of Hampshire. Arabella's papa, Viscount Vaughn, was also of a respected old family. Yes, the harpies agreed, Arabella was an impressive alliance for Lord Estes, whose dying father, after all, was as disreputable as he was rich.

"The countess Henrietta must be overjoyed at the earl's imminent demise," the harpy dubbed Lady Snide observed. "I know of no husband and wife who cherish a greater hatred for each other."

All the world knew that Woodthorpe, a notorious rake, had abandoned his countess for an Irish light-skirt who had also borne him a son. The earl doted upon this by-blow, who was said to be even wilder and more reckless than his sire.

The three harpies fell temporarily silent as Arabella passed by, accompanied by her sister, stepmother, and aunt, the duchess of Hampshire. Arabella's simple white muslin gown and her sister's blue were as pretty as they were tasteful. But their stepmother was arrayed in a puce satin so crowded with brilliants, ribbons, and ruffles that it was eye-popping on her overblown figure, although not in the way the lady thought.

Whatever, asked the harpies, could have possessed Lord Vaughn to marry such a vulgar, odious woman, nearer in age to his daughters than to himself? And to marry her so quickly—only six months—after the death of his first wife, whom he had adored.

The first Lady Vaughn had been a legendary beauty, and Beth was the image of her: a tiny, fragile wisp with a halo of glorious blond curls surrounding a delicate face set with wide azure eyes, a slightly upturned nose, and a delectable little mouth. Arabella and Beth shared the same pert nose and brilliant eyes. But Arabella, who was almost nineteen and a year older, was a half head taller and fuller of face and figure. Instead of obedient blond curls, Arabella's hair was a mass of defiant chestnut waves.

The sisters were equally different in personalities. Arabella had inherited her mama's: so high-spirited, impetuous, and shockingly forthright that at times she bordered on the outrageous. But Beth, despite her beauty, was timid and quiet.

A moment after the Vaughn party took seats on a long yellow banquette not far from the harpies, Lord Estes appeared at the ballroom entrance. Although he was short and tended toward the portly, he was undeniably handsome, and his splendid raiment proclaimed him a tulip of fashion. He moved with the languid haughtiness of an aristocrat accustomed since birth to having others bow and scrape to him.

Seeing him, the duchess of Hampshire frowned and said to her nieces, "It's shocking."

"What is?" the girls' stepmother demanded.

The duchess had been pointedly ignoring Lady Vaughn, who had insisted on accompanying Her Grace tonight even though she had not been invited. Neither the duchess's blunt tongue nor her undisguised dislike of Lady Vaughn could defeat Her Ladyship's determination to be seen publicly in Her Grace's company. Nor was Lady Vaughn a woman who permitted herself to be ignored. It was by such tenacity that she had managed to rise to viscountess from her humble origins as the daughter of a poor country parson.

When the duchess did not answer her, Lady Vaughn persisted. "What's shocking?"

"That Lord Estes is so cordially hated by his dying father that Woodthorpe refuses even to see his only legitimate son and heir," the duchess said. "Instead Woodthorpe keeps his Irish by-blow by his deathbed."

"Surely, Aunt Margaret," a startled Arabella protested, "that cannot be true."

Lady Vaughn said coldly, "It is to Lord Estes's credit that he is not close to that evil earl who so openly flaunted his despicable morals." She gave a loud, disapproving sniff. "I am not surprised that Woodthorpe prefers his by-blow. They are two of a kind. I've heard that Woodthorpe even tried to buy the wretch a place in society by marrying him to the daughter of a poor but prestigious family." Lady Vaughn gave another disapproving sniff. "Of course, he did not succeed."

"Lord Estes has said nothing to me about his father's being so ill," Arabella said. "What is wrong with him?"

"I am told it is some mysterious, wasting malady that struck him down very suddenly," the duchess replied.

Lord Estes stepped inside the ballroom. He was immediately stopped by Lady Lewis and her lovely young daughter, Mary, who had been dangling after him all season to no avail.

Arabella was sincerely amazed that Estes should prefer her to the lovely Miss Lewis. With the incomparable Beth as Arabella's standard, she erroneously thought herself large, awkward, and very plain—not that Arabella was the least bit envious of Beth. She adored her sweet, shy sister.

Arabella watched in fascination as Miss Lewis demurely fluttered her silk fan and smiled coyly at Lord Estes over it. Not being at all coquettish, Arabella could never manage to simper over an eligible male as Miss Lewis did nor to mold her opinions to fit his. Nor could she seem to curb her frank tongue and irreverent humor, despite her stepmother's incessant lectures that she totally lacked the decorum and feminine wiles necessary to ensnare a man.

Certainly Arabella had not tried to ensnare Estes, had not even paid him much heed initially, and most certainly had not fawned over him as other girls did. It never occurred to Arabella that her disinterest might have been a powerful attraction to a man who had been besieged by almost every other nubile female in London.

Lady Vaughn had been as confounded as the three harpies by Lord Estes's interest in her stepdaughter and had repeatedly assured Arabella that she was wholly undeserving of this singular honor.

Although Lord Estes clearly preferred Arabella's company, he had given no hint whether his interest was so well fixed that he would make her an offer. Arabella was eager for him to do so. He was the only man whom she had met that she had the slightest interest in marrying.

Lady Vaughn, her greedy eyes fixed on Estes, said to the duchess, "Dear Lord Estes is such a pleasing young man, so unlike his father."

"Pleasing!" scoffed Her Grace, who was famous—and feared—for her outspokenness. "What is pleasing about a sullen young scamp who spends his time at the gaming tables losing money he does not have? If I were the earl, I would not want Estes around me either."

Lord Estes was a special favorite of Lady Vaughn's, and she rushed to defend him. "Lord Estes can afford to lose a few pounds. His father is one of the richest men in England."

"And to remain so, the earl had to refuse to pay any more of Lord Estes's gambling debts," the duchess replied caustically. "Not that this inconvenience has stopped him. He's been living on his expectations and what his mother can give him. It's said, though, that she has very nearly gone through her own considerable fortune."

Arabella was shocked by these revelations about Estes. "Why have you never told me of his gambling or his father's animosity toward him before, Aunt Margaret?" her niece asked reproachfully.

"I only just learned of them myself. The earl and I have the same solicitor. When I asked him today whether the rumor that Woodthorpe refuses to see his heir is true, he said that it is and that they fell out over Estes's huge gambling losses."

Still that struck Arabella as insufficient reason for a dying man to refuse to see his son. Poor Estes must be devastated.

Beth, who was sitting beside Arabella on the banquette, gave a sudden start and stared with glowing eyes at the doorway. Standing there was her adored lieutenant, Justin Keats, a tall, handsome young man of two and twenty with a strong, square face and frank blue eyes that seemed incapable of deception.

The exquisite Beth had attracted a legion of suitors, many of them far more eligible than Justin. But once she had met him, no other man had existed for her. To Lady Vaughn's fury, Beth's other beaux, seeing the way the wind blew, had gradually drifted away.

Justin's eyes discovered Beth. From the sudden happiness that shone on his face, Arabella was once again reassured that his love for Beth was at least as intense as hers was for him. A flower of Beth's rare beauty and fragility needed just such a kind, loving man as the lieutenant to protect and cherish her. A stern, insensitive husband without great sensibility would soon trample Beth's delicate spirit.

Arabella offered up a silent prayer that Lady Vaughn would not be able to thwart the impecunious lieutenant's suit. If Beth and Justin were separated, Arabella was certain that her sister, whose health was as frail as her form, would go into a decline that could kill her.

The orchestra began playing, dancers moved onto the floor, and Justin strode purposefully toward Beth.

"I will have this dance, Miss Beth," a grating voice at Beth's elbow said.

Both sisters started. Neither had noticed the approach of Rufus Dobbs, a middle-aged, self-made man of great wealth and equally great but unrealized social ambitions. He reminded Arabella of an aging, ugly bulldog with his surly disposition; heavy, flabby body; and a face that seemed all jowls. Beth could not suppress a tiny shudder of revulsion at the sight of him.

Lady Vaughn bestowed upon Dobbs her largest smile. "Of course you shall, Mr. Dobbs. Beth is delighted." When her dazed stepdaughter did not move, Her Ladyship ordered her sharply to go with him.

Reluctantly Beth did so. As Dobbs led her away, she cast an agonized look at Justin. He stopped abruptly, the joy in his eyes fading to disappointment.

Arabella could hardly contain her anger at her stepmother. When Dobbs had first been introduced by Lady Vaughn at the beginning of the season, she had treated him with the frigidity he merited. But as the Vaughns' financial difficulties mounted, her coldness had given way to increasing warmth.

The duchess said sharply, "I am shocked that you would permit Beth to dance with that odious toad. He is so excessively beneath her."

Lady Vaughn picked nervously at the lace ruffle trimming the wrist of her gown. "He is such a dear man and so exceedingly fond of Beth," she began defensively.

"He is an ugly boor of despicable origins and older than Beth's father," snapped the duchess. "And her beauty, great as it is, does not fix his interest half so much as her connections. He can never hope to achieve his social ambitions except by marrying someone like Beth, who is related, principally through *her mother,* to most of the great families of England.''

This pointed reminder that the first Lady Vaughn, the duchess's sister, had been far superior to the second brought an angry flush to Her Ladyship's face. "I find Mr. Dobbs a fine gentleman." Lady Vaughn's final two words trailed off feebly, for even she had difficulty with such an enormous lie.

The duchess fixed Lady Vaughn with her famous look—the one of ineffable contempt that unfailingly reduced lesser souls to quivering jelly and had even quelled a few lords of the highest rank. "You and he are both social-climbing schemers, cut from the same greedy cloth.''

Her Ladyship's face turned the color of her puce gown. She jumped up and rushed away through a clot of interested observers.

Arabella would have felt sorry for her stepmother had it not been for the enormous unhappiness that she had brought to the Vaughn family. In truth, she was exactly what the duchess had said. Her Ladyship had trapped Lord Vaughn, still buried in grief over the death of Arabella's beloved mama, into marrying her; had plunged him so deeply into debt with her gambling and other wild extravagances that he faced financial ruin; and had turned his only son, Arabella's twin brother, Bromley, from a happy, high-spirited youth into a sullen rebel.

"I cannot image why Lady Pyne would have invited Mr. Dobbs here tonight," Arabella said to her aunt.

The duchess shrugged. "It's rumored that she is not too well to pass at the moment and this affair is costing a pretty pound. Dobbs is a man used to buying his way. I suspect he is paying much of the bill in exchange for the privilege of attending.''

Arabella watched her sister as she moved gracefully about the dance floor. "Dear Beth is so beautiful, isn't she," Arabella said proudly.

The duchess gave her niece an amused smile. The modest Arabella was wholly unaware of her own loveliness. She did not know how beguiling were the dimples that flashed in her cheeks. Nor did she realize that her azure eyes sparkled with an enticing spirit that her demure sister's lacked.

"Your Grace," a man's voice said, "will you permit me to stand up with your niece for this dance?"

It was Lord Estes, a smile that did not seem to touch his slate-blue eyes playing upon his thin lips. He prided himself on his sartorial elegance, and tonight he was resplendent in a violet satin frock coat edged with ruffles over white breeches. His stockings were of striped silk, and his black pumps sported gold buckles. His white satin waistcoat was embroidered with gold thread, and a huge amethyst glittered in the folds of his perfectly arranged lace cravat.

The width of the violet satin shoulders and the nipped-in waist hinted that the former were padded and the latter was corseted. The careful arrangement of blond curls around his face bespoke a curling iron and a patient valet. In truth, Arabella preferred less peacockishness in male toilet, but she could not deny that Lord Estes's attire was all the crack among the more exquisite pinks of the ton.

The dance was a cotillion that would give Arabella little opportunity to talk to Estes. As he led her onto the floor, he said, "When this dance is over, I want to find a quiet corner. I have something of utmost importance to ask you."

Arabella's heart leaped. Perhaps at last he would make her an offer. She had been taught that the getting of a husband was the chief business of a woman's life, but for one of her lineage not just any husband would suit. It had been impressed upon her almost from the cradle that marriage to a social inferior was unthinkable, a betrayal of her distinguished family and all those generations of forebears who had forged her impeccable pedigree. So it was hardly surprising that Arabella, who was devoid of vanity about herself, was flattered by the interest of such a sought-after prize as Lord Estes.

Not that Arabella entertained for Estes the passionate, all-consuming love that her sister harbored for Justin Keats. But having reached the advanced age of nearly nineteen without ever experiencing such passion, Arabella was convinced that the fault lay with herself. She was not at all romantic. Her eye for amusing imperfections was too keen for her to abandon herself to an uncritical adoration of even such a prime catch as Lord Estes. Nevertheless, he interested her more than the other men she had met, and she had convinced herself that this meant she cared for him as much as she could for any man.

And Arabella was anxious to marry. She wanted no more London seasons. She was tired of both town and ton, tired of being laced to the point of suffocation into gowns that were as uncomfortable to wear as they were beautiful to look at, and tired of the severe constraints on speech and behavior imposed on unmarried young ladies of quality.

She longed for the freedom of the country, where she could put aside her stays, ride recklessly across the fields, and comb the woods for new secrets of nature. It was Arabella's fondest hope that if she married Estes, she could persuade him to live permanently at Woodthorpe Hall, his country estate in Yorkshire.

If only she had been a boy, Arabella thought as she moved through the intricate pattern of the cotillion. Ever her indifferent papa, who generally took no notice of his children, said that she had the bottom of one and was pluck to the backbone.

She rode with the abandon and seat of an out-and-outer, never flinching at the highest fence or the trickiest jump. She was a notable whip, handling a four-in-hand with the skill of a nonpareil.

How different a child she had been from Beth, who had cowered in the dark and at the strange sounds in the woods.

Arabella had not feared either. Indeed, she had often displayed more courage and daring than her twin brother in their childhood adventures and pranks. Certainly she had climbed trees with greater agility than Brom. Her hoydenish ways had dismayed her papa and delighted her mama, who had understood because she had seen in her daughter a mirror of herself as a child.

But those happy days had ended with Lord Vaughn's remarriage. His second wife had been determined to remold Arabella into a model of simpering propriety and had succeeded only in making her stepdaughter's life miserable.

When the cotillion ended, Estes led Arabella through the ballroom's french doors onto the terrace. Inside, the orchestra struck up a country reel, and Arabella was delighted to see Lieutenant Keats claim Beth from Dobbs.

To Arabella's surprise, she also saw Peter Bosley, a notorious gamester, walking resolutely toward Estes and her.

Estes saw him, too. "Damn," he muttered, then said to her, "Pray excuse me. I just recollected a most pressing engagement."

With that, he stepped heavily off the terrace and vanished into the darkness.

Behind her, Bosley demanded, "Where did Lord Estes go?"

"I don't know," Arabella said, clearly perplexed.

"Lord Estes is avoiding me," Bosley explained. "He owes me a very large debt of honor."

The confirmation of what her aunt had said about Lord Estes's gambling dismayed Arabella, and she longed for a quiet spot in which to ponder what she had learned about him tonight.

Bosley offered to return Arabella to the ballroom, but she declined, saying she preferred the fresh air. He bowed and left her.

Seeking privacy, she walked slowly to the end of the terrace, bathed in dark shadows, where she would be less likely to be noticed. As Arabella stood there, a quiet voice drifted out on the night air:

"It will be exceedingly difficult for me to persuade her father to marry such a diamond of the first water to you." Arabella recognized her stepmother's voice. "The price will be very high."

"I will pay whatever is necessary—I am a very rich man," Rufus Dobbs's guttural voice replied. "I am used to buying what I want, and I mean to have Beth as my wife."

Arabella clamped her hands over her mouth to suppress the cry of rage that sprang up in her throat. Was there no end to her stepmother's evil scheming?

Lady Vaughn said bluntly, "If I am to win her father's agreement to your marriage, I must be recompensed, too."

"You will be richly rewarded *if your efforts are successful*," Dobbs assured her.

"It will be in addition to what you give my husband," Lady Vaughn said. "He must know nothing of your payment to me."

Arabella clenched her fists in fury. That diabolical woman! If Lady Vaughn succeeded in forcing poor, fragile Beth to marry Dobbs, it would kill her.

But Lady Vaughn would *not* succeed! Arabella swore solemnly to herself that she would, she *must*, find a way to thwart her stepmother and to assure Beth's marriage to Justin. Beth's life depended upon it!

Chapter 2

Arabella's vow to do anything to assure Beth's marriage to Justin was put to the test the very next night.

The sisters spent the day at their cousins', the duke of Lysted's daughters. Once Arabella and Beth had escaped their stepmother's oppressive company, they had not been anxious to return, so darkness was falling before the duke's carriage brought them back to the Vaughn residence in Arlington Street.

Arabella was uncharacteristically quiet on the return ride. One of her cousins, Lady Elizabeth, had taken Arabella aside and confided to her a shocking tale: Arabella's twin brother, Bromley, had fallen wildly in love with a young demirep.

"My brother, Lance, says there is something very smoky about it," Lady Elizabeth said. "Brom told him that her name is Julie Berner. But Lance is certain that she is really Julia Coates, who is a notorious highflier. Lance says she looks fifteen and as innocent as an angel, but she's nearly a decade older. She ran away from home when she was fifteen to live under the protection of Lord Black, whose reputation is the same as his name. Since then she has had a series of other very rich, sophisticated protectors. Lance tried to tell your brother that, but Brom would not believe him and became so angry that he nearly gave Lance a facer. Has Brom talked to you about her?''

Arabella shook her head sadly. She and Brom had always been so close until their father had remarried, but now she hardly saw him. Lady Vaughn's vituperative treatment had so alienated him that he rarely was home. When he was, their stepmother seemed always to be hovering about, making it difficult for the brother and sister to talk privately.

"But why would this Julia lie about who she is?" Arabella asked.

Lady Elizabeth frowned. "Lance thinks it is because she is afraid that if Brom knew her real identity, he would not marry her.''

"Marry her!" Arabella was aghast. "Surely Brom cannot be—''

"He told Lance that she has accepted his offer,'' Lady Elizabeth said. "What Lance cannot understand is why, if she is Julia Coates, she would have done so. She cares only for rich, sophisticated men of the world, who can indulge her expensive tastes, not naive, penniless eighteen-year-olds like Brom.''

"Then what on earth can she possibly want with him?" Arabella asked.

She was still asking herself the same question when the duke's carriage stopped in front of her home in Arlington Street. Arabella had been commanded by her dying mama, who knew her husband's indolence and disinterest in his children, to watch over Beth and Brom. Arabella had tried hard to comply with Mama's charge, but she felt inadequate to deal with Brom's latest involvement.

As a footman opened the carriage door for the sisters to alight, Arabella noticed a lanky young man loitering in the shadows. When Beth descended from the carriage, he dashed up to her, thrust a note into her hand, and vanished around the corner before either surprised sister could find her tongue.

Arabella was the first to recover. "Wasn't that Justin Keats's lackey?"

Beth, clutching the note tightly, nodded.

As they entered the house, Tynes, the butler, looked about furtively as though he expected Lady Vaughn to materialize at any instant. Passing close to Arabella, he muttered so that only she could hear, "Talk to your abigail at once." Then he hastily disappeared into the drawing room.

Beth had already started up the stairs, unsealing the note as she went. When the two sisters reached the bedroom that they shared, Beth immediately unfolded the sheet and began reading it. The sisters' abigail, Jane, appeared in the door just as Beth gave a strangled cry and collapsed to the floor in a dead faint.

Kneeling beside Beth's still form, Arabella demanded, "What happened while we were out?"

The abigail's words tumbled out in a disjointed stream, but Arabella was able to glean that Lieutenant Keats had come to see Beth because his regiment had received unexpected orders. It was to depart at dawn the next morning to join the duke of Wellington's army on the Continent.

Justin had been greeted by Lady Vaughn with a brutal canard. She had assured him that although Beth was at home, she had no desire to see him now or ever again. Beth was a beautiful flirt who had merely been leading him on for a lark. Now, realizing how deeply he felt about her, she was too embarrassed to face him with the truth and so asked her stepmother to deliver the message for her.

"Surely Justin did not believe her," Arabella said.

"Tynes said Lady Vaughn was so convincing that he almost believed her himself, and he knows how much Miss Beth loves Lieutenant Keats. Tynes said that the poor lieutenant rushed out of the house as though the fires of hell were aburning him.''

A moan escaped from Beth's lips and her eyes slowly opened. Arabella and Jane helped her to her bed. The letter that had had such a profound effect upon her was still clutched in her hand. Slowly she held it out to Arabella, her eyes deep pools of misery and confusion.

"I cannot comprehend what Justin writes me. It makes no sense.''

Arabella took the sheet and scanned its contents, which confirmed that Justin had believed her stepmother's lies. The letter had been written while he was still reeling with shock and disillusionment. Gripped in a white heat of anger and grief, he had poured into it his confounded, seething emotions and concluded by saying that Beth was sending him off to war having robbed him of any reason for returning alive.

Taking Beth's cold hands in her own, Arabella explained what Lady Vaughn had told Justin. Beth shrieked and began to cry hysterically.

Clutching frantically at her sister, Beth sobbed, "What am I to do? He cannot go off to war thinking that I care naught for him. Oh, Arabella, I want to die, too! I shall die!'' Beth trembled as though seized by a great chill. Her face turned as white as the pillow on which her head rested. "I cannot bear to live without Justin.''

Much later, Arabella was still trying to soothe her distraught sister when Lady Vaughn's maid knocked on the door to tell them that they were to leave with her in an hour for Lady James's drum.

"Tell her that we will not be accompanying her tonight,'' Arabella called through the door. "Beth is very ill, and I cannot leave her.''

To Arabella's relief, Lady Vaughn did not come to inquire about her stepdaughter before going out. Beth was still crying, and Arabella feared that the sight of their stepmother would only upset Beth more.

As the evening passed, Arabella grew more and more apprehensive about her sister, who refused food and became increasingly feverish. Feeling Beth's hot forehead, Arabella thought frantically, she *will* die if Justin leaves on the morrow thinking she does not love him.

In desperation, Arabella grasped Beth's hands and said, "We will get a message to Justin tonight telling him of Lady Vaughn's lies and reassuring him of your love."

"But who will carry it?" Beth whispered weakly. "Justin's regiment is billeted so far away—on the other side of Hounslow Heath. And he leaves at dawn."

"Brom will take it," Arabella said, even though she had very little hope of seeing her brother tonight. He would undoubtedly stay with his friend Elton Davies, because Lord Vaughn was at his cousin's in Sussex. When papa was gone, Brom was never seen in Arlington Street, having quickly learned that Lady Vaughn would rip at him incessantly, dwelling in exquisite detail upon every fault, both real and imagined, that she could find. And Lady Vaughn could readily have found a myriad of faults in the most saintly of souls. Not that Brom was any saint, and since acquiring her as his stepmother, he had become steadily less so.

"Oh, Arabella, Brom is just the one," Beth cried. "He will be able to convince Justin." Her face puckered in concern. "But Brom must find someone to ride with him. It would be too dangerous for him to go alone."

Arabella recognized as clearly as Beth the dangers involved in crossing Hounslow Heath. It was a haven for highwaymen, the most notorious of whom, Big Bart Bailey and his brother, Squint, were suspected in the murders of a half-dozen hapless travelers there, and a substantial reward had been offered for their capture.

"Only last week," Beth was saying, "Lord Dundee's

armed groom was shot and badly wounded on the heath by a
highwayman who forced the coach to stop. The wretched
thief robbed His Lordship of everything, even ripping the
gold buckles from his shoes and the gold buttons from his
coat. Brom must be very careful.''

"He will be," Arabella reassured her. "Don't you worry
about him. Now, my dearest Beth, you are quite worn-out.
Let me prepare you a *tisane*."

"I cannot think of sleeping until I know that Justin—"

"No, of course not," Arabella said, "but it will soothe
you."

And to make certain that it not only soothed Beth but put
her to sleep, Arabella secretly added a bit of laudanum. Soon
Beth drifted into a restless, feverish sleep.

Arabella was reminded of the long nights that she had spent
at her sister's bedside two years ago when Beth had been
stricken with scarlet fever. She had not been expected to live,
but Arabella, who had not left her sister's side for ten days,
had nursed her through it in place of their mama, who had
been dying of consumption. Although Beth had recovered,
the illness had exacted a permanent toll. She had to avoid any
stress on her weakened heart and her constitution. If Justin
departed at dawn without knowing the truth, Arabella was
terrified that the grief and strain would kill Beth.

Arabella could not let that happen. But whom on earth
could she get to carry the message? She had no hope that
Brom would return. She thought of trying to bribe a servant
but rejected this as hopeless. Not one of them would have the
courage to cross Hounslow Heath at night.

Time crept slowly by, and Arabella heard a clock strike
ten. The house was very quiet now. All of the servants had
retired belowstairs. She placed her hand on her sister's hot
forehead. Her fever was rising.

In despair, Arabella hit upon a scheme so wild and crazy
that she dared not let herself even think about it or its possible

consequences. Before her courage could fail her, she hurried down the hall to Brom's chamber. Hastily she pulled out his buckskin riding breeches, well-polished hessian boots, cambric shirt, and riding coat, and put them on. As she did so, she told herself over and over that she could not let Beth die.

Fortunately Brom was slender, so his breeches fit Arabella rather better than she had expected. But his boots were too large, and she was forced to stuff handkerchiefs into the toes. She swept up her long hair into a coil and concealed it beneath her brother's hat.

The chimes of Big Ben were striking when a slim figure wrapped in a long riding coat crept down the back stairs and out a rear door of Lord Vaughn's to his stable behind the house.

Arabella dared not summon a groom to help her. Nor could she use a sidesaddle that would betray her sex. She went to the stall of Gray Charger, the big gelding that was the fastest horse in the stable. Quickly she saddled him, mounted, and rode into a black, moonless night.

Although it was warm, she pulled the scarf that she wore around her neck up about her face. Between the scarf and the brim of her hat, the feminine cast of her features was well concealed.

At first she held the gray to a slow trot, keeping in the shadows of residential streets that, to her relief, were deserted. As she reached the outskirts of the city, Arabella increased her pace. The houses and the safety they represented grew more and more infrequent and the night blacker.

She fought down her growing unease by reminding herself how crucial her mission was to Beth. Arabella wondered what it would be like to love a man as her sister did Justin. Surely if Arabella could not love Lord Estes like that, she could not any man.

Although she was disturbed by what her aunt had said the previous night about His Lordship, Arabella quieted her doubts by ticking off Estes's virtues to herself: He was handsome, although his slate-blue eyes sometimes seemed to Arabella to be too appraising and disdainful of his fellow creatures. He was intelligent and not at all transparent like her other suitors, who plied her with compliments clothed in ridiculous hyperbole and betrayed with their own tongues their dullness or foolishness.

Lord Estes neither paid Arabella compliments nor bored her with interminable stories about himself. He talked little about himself or, for that matter, anything else. He preferred to listen to Arabella's forthright, amusing comments instead. He constantly sought her out at balls, routs, and assemblies, but he never took her riding in the park or called on her in Arlington Street, where they might have had more intimate conversations than were possible at large gatherings.

In truth, Lord Estes was an enigma to Arabella. Had she refined much upon it, she might have realized that this was what interested her about him. But she did not refine upon it, for she was anxious to be married and free of Lady Vaughn's tyranny.

As Arabella rode on through the dark, the clouds occasionally parted, allowing the light of a three-quarter moon to illuminate the way. Then the rolling gray billows covered the moon and blackness descended again.

When she neared Hounslow Heath, the most treacherous part of her journey, she could no longer hold her fear in check. The full madness and danger of the scheme she was undertaking hit her and very nearly undermined her determination. She thought of Big Bart Bailey and of Lord Dundee's recent experience. Her hands crept unconsciously to a button on Brom's coat. She was relieved to feel that it was of cloth and not precious metal. Should a highwayman rob her, he would get little for his trouble. Not only were her buttons not gold, but her boots had no buckles, her person no jewels, and her pocket but ten shillings.

Never before in her life had she regretted her impetuosity so much as she did at this moment. She tried to reassure herself that Gray Charger could surely outrun any highwayman's mount and that the greater danger to her tonight was not from bandits but from the sharp eyes of Lieutenant Keats's fellow officers. While her disguise was sufficient for a rider in the dark, it was doubtful that it would fool any hussar who might see her up close in the lamplight. Nor had she any idea how she could contrive a secret audience with Justin once she reached the quarters that he shared with several other officers.

She dared not even contemplate the scandal that would ensue should she be recognized. She would be ruined, all chance of an advantageous match—or any marriage at all—gone forever. Lord Estes, so conscious of his own consequence, would never choose as his future countess a hoyden who galloped alone across the dark countryside, dressed like a man and riding like one as well, to visit the quarters of a bachelor army officer.

Reaching the heath, Arabella urged Gray Charger to a full gallop. The clouds over the moon had temporarily thinned to a light veil, and for the first half mile she could make out her way fairly well amid the lousewort, bog pimpernel, and low mounds of heather that stretched along the heath like miniature hills. Then the clouds thickened, obliterating both the faint light and her resolve.

By now she appreciated the enormous folly of her errand and the consequences that could be its legacy. A chill shook her slender frame that had nothing to do with cold, for it was a warm night, far too warm to have one's face cloaked in a heavy scarf.

Arabella's common sense told her that her journey was hopeless. Her courage faltered. She must go back.

But Beth's pallid face, bathed in misery, rose up in Arabella's memory. The thought of having to tell Beth on the morrow that Justin had gone to war thinking her a heartless deceiver was unbearable to Arabella, and she did not turn back. She had vowed that she would do anything to aid her beloved sister, and by heaven above, so she would, whatever the cost to herself. Arabella, her teeth chattering, plunged on across the notorious heath.

The harsh startling cry of a night bird pierced the darkness, tearing a frightened sob from Arabella's throat. An answering cry came, then several more, as though the birds were warning of a danger lurking somewhere in the darkness of the heath.

Arabella thought she heard another noise ahead of her. She strained her ears but could make out nothing more than the raucous birdcalls.

Across the heath, a pinprick of light flickered from a far lantern, no doubt mounted on a carriage traveling toward her. The tiny dot comforted her, making her feel less alone.

Suddenly ahead of her, from a clump of bushes that were but a vague outline in the dark, a shadow leaped out and a brawny arm grabbed for Gray Charger's bridle. Instantly Arabella veered her horse, and the big hand closed on empty air.

Terrified, Arabella dug her heels hard into Gray Charger, urging him on. The big gelding lunged forward with a burst of speed. She guided him toward the dot of light still flickering in the distance and prayed that she might reach it before the highwayman could catch her.

Behind her, she heard a hoarse voice cursing violently. Her assailant's lunge for her bridle coupled with her unexpected maneuver had thrown him momentarily off-balance. It was all the time that Arabella and Gray Charger needed to increase the distance from the furious voice.

He yelled, " 'Alt, or me'll shoot ya dead.''

Arabella shook with terror, but she urged her mount on. Surely the highwayman could not see her well enough in the dark to hit her. She preferred the risk of being wounded to the certainty of what would happen if she stopped. The bandit's cursing grew fainter.

But then the accursed clouds drifted away from the face of the half-moon. To Arabella's horror, she suddenly found herself bathed in its pale light and a much clearer target for her pursuer.

" 'Alt,'' the man yelled again, "or me lead will 'alt ya.''

Arabella hunched down over Gray Charger's neck. She heard a loud explosion and something whizzed very close over her head. The ball struck the ground a little ahead of the gelding, kicking up a shower of dirt.

She was shaking violently now, but still she kept going. She raised her head slightly to make certain that she was still headed toward the light, but it had vanished! She had no idea where it had gone or toward what she was now headed. Despair engulfed her, and she fought down her panic.

Another explosion roared. A second bullet sped past her arm and ripped through the leaves of a low shrub not more than a foot from her horse's left hoof.

A row of bog myrtle bushes loomed ahead. As she reached it, a horse raced from the protective cover toward her. Thinking that aid was at hand, Arabella's spirits soared.

"Help," she screamed at the top of her voice. "Help me!"

But instead of doing so, the rider grabbed for Gray Charger's bridle and began forcing the big gelding to check its speed.

Arabella realized in terror and despair how wrong she had been in thinking that rescue was at hand. The second rider was another highwayman. She screamed again for help even though she knew there would be none for her in the empty darkness. It was midnight by now and highly unlikely that anyone with honest motives would be crossing the notorious heath.

Her original pursuer rode up on the other side of Gray Charger, and the two bandits forced her mount to a halt. The men jumped down from their horses and ordered Arabella to do the same. She remained stubbornly in the saddle. She was determined that they should not suspect how terrified she was. In the moonlight, she could see that both men wore masks to conceal their faces. Both were brawny, but her first pursuer was taller than the second by several inches.

The bigger man said, " 'E must 'ave a pile a blunt on 'im ta lead me on the chase 'e did."

"You will be sadly disappointed," Arabella told them in as deep a voice as she could manage, hoping to preserve her disguise as a man. "I have no money or valuables at all."

" 'Ah, and the king, he don't have no crown either," the second man jeered. He pulled a small pistol from his belt and pointed it at Arabella. Squinting up at her, he said to his larger companion, " 'E's a young 'un, ain't 'e now, Bart. Come on, boy, 'op down right quicklike."

Arabella did not move. The big man, who she suspected must be the infamous Bart Bailey, reached up and unceremoniously yanked her from the saddle, letting her fall bruisingly to the ground. Brom's hat fell off her head. The great mass of chestnut hair that she had coiled beneath it escaped the pins and tumbled down about her shoulders.

"Gawd," Bart exclaimed, " 'e be a 'er, Squint."

"Aye," Squint agreed. He tore away the heavy scarf from around Arabella's face and neck to reveal the feminine contours of her face. "And a right bold piece 'er be." He waved his pistol at her. "Empty out your pockets, m'lady, and be quick about it."

She did as she was ordered. When the two men discovered that she had but ten shillings and no jewelry or other valuables, they both cursed violently.

"To think we was led on such a chase for ten shillings," Bart fumed, stuffing his pistol into his belt. He grabbed Arabella by the front of Brom's coat and jerked her toward him.

"Ya give me one kinda ride for nothin', m'lady, so now me's gonna give you another kind to make it worth me trouble."

She stared at him uncomprehendingly. Arabella had been raised in deliberate, sheltered ignorance of certain facts of life. As a result, she had only a vague and most romantic idea of what occurred between a man and a woman, and no notion at all of the darker side of lust. She had been carefully instructed in the proprieties that she must observe, such as never being alone with a man or permitting him to kiss her, but because she had been given no real explanation for these edicts, they seemed as silly to her as all other tiresome rules, such as being required to ride sidesaddle, that were imposed upon young ladies of quality.

Although Arabella did not understand what Bart was talking about, the look on his face as he stepped toward her terrified her, and she screamed again for help.

"Scream your 'ead off," Bart told her. "Ain't nobody out on the 'eath to 'ear you."

"But you are wrong," said a strong deep voice very nearby.

Arabella and her captors gaped as a figure stepped from between the bog myrtle. Arabella's first impression was that he was a man of heroic proportions, rather like a Michelangelo sculpture, tall, broad, and powerfully built with rippling muscles. He wore buckskin riding breeches and a spencer of impeccable tailoring but no riding coat. In each hand, he held a pistol aimed at the highwaymen.

"Gawd, where'd 'e drop from?" Bart asked in awe. "Never 'eard a sound. And 'im such a big 'un, too."

Squint wasted no time on words. He whirled upon the newcomer with his pistol. The gun in the stranger's left hand belched fire, and Squint crumpled to the ground.

As Arabella stared down at the fallen bandit, Bart grabbed her and pulled her in front of him to shield himself from the unfired gun in the stranger's right hand.

"Shoot at me, and it'll be 'er you 'it," Bart told him. The bandit then addressed his fallen companion. "How be ye, Squint?"

"He be dead, you fool," the stranger replied calmly. "Which is what you will be unless you unhand the girl."

"Nay, 'er and me, we be going for ride," Bart said. He tightened his grip on Arabella and forced her to edge backward with him toward his horse.

Chapter 3

Arabella, seeing deliverance snatched from her, tried frantically to break Bart's hold on her as he used her body to shield his own. She clawed at his arm and kicked at him furiously with Brom's hessian boots, but to no avail.

"Release the girl, and I shall let you live," the stranger said calmly, returning the pistol with which he had shot Squint to his belt. The unfired gun in his right hand remained leveled steadily at Arabella. "Otherwise, I will kill you."

Bart's only answer was a pungent comment on the circumstances of the stranger's birth. The bandit continued to force Arabella back. She knew the stranger dared not carry out his threat to fire while Bart held her in front of him.

She heard the neigh of a horse only a few feet behind her. Desperate that the highwayman would succeed in escaping with her, she suddenly jerked and let her full weight fall forward just as Bart was taking a step backward. Her unexpected maneuver caught him both off-guard and off-balance. They tumbled forward, and she landed on the ground hard beneath him.

She tensed waiting for a shot, but none came. Why didn't the stranger fire? Bart now made an excellent target.

The bandit must have realized this, too, for he scrambled

hastily to his feet and leaped for his horse. Only then did the shot ring out. The ball caught him in midair, and for a second he hung suspended there before plunging to earth.

Slowly Arabella raised her head, propped it on her trembling elbow, and stared at Bart's body. "Is he dead?" she quavered.

"But of course," the stranger said calmly, pocketing the second pistol. "I am a man of my word. Are you hurt?"

She shook her head. "Only terrified."

He bent over her, lifted her up with gentle hands, and carried her through the bog myrtle so that it screened the bodies from her sight.

The reassuring strength of his arms undermined the last shreds of Arabella's composure. As he restored her to her feet, she began to shake violently.

"You are safe now," her rescuer told her soothingly, holding her comfortingly close. Her first impression of him—that he was a rugged mountain of a man—was confirmed now that she stood beside him. Arabella was a tall woman, but she was a full head shorter than he was.

Though chattering teeth, she stammered, "I am sorry to be so foolish, but I cannot help it."

"I do not think you foolish but very brave." His voice was soft, deep, and reassuring.

"No, I am very pudding-hearted," Arabella contradicted. "My heart is knocking against my ribs, and I cannot stop shaking."

Her frankness brought a gleam of admiration to his dark eyes. "I am impressed by a woman who, when she is captured by highwaymen, does not dissolve immediately into strong hysterics."

"Oh, I am not *that* pudding-hearted! And I had to keep my wits about me if I were to have any hope of saving myself."

"You are undoubtedly right. But I can think of no woman

of my current acquaintance who could manage such admirable restraint,'' he said with an approving grin.

She blushed at his praise and was suddenly intensely curious about him. "You are very cool. Do you kill a man or two every day?"

"Hardly. But the world is better off without those two scoundrels. I am certain that I have just rid Hounslow Heath of the notorious Big Bart and Squint Bailey.''

The clouds slid away from the moon so that it again spilled its pale light on the heath and illuminated Arabella's tall rescuer. His muscular shoulders were the widest she had ever seen, and below them his strong body tapered to slim hips in buckskin breeches. His spencer, shirt, and elegantly arranged cravat were of the finest materials. Standing before him, Arabella had the irrational feeling that she was safely in the shadow of a proud, unassilable mountain that would shelter her.

But it was his aristocratic face that most intrigued her: it was as strong as his body, with sharp angles and planes that began with a broad forehead and culminated in the jutting point of a rock-hard chin. His mouth was sensuous, and his deep-set eyes, dark beneath thick, triangular eyebrows, had a riveting quality about them. Thick, straight hair appeared black in the pale moonlight, and his complexion, too, was dark. She was uncertain of his age but believed him to be in his early thirties. He was, Arabella decided, the most handsome man she had ever seen.

He returned her scrutiny with a curiosity as lively as her own. She was startled to see his dark eyes turn hard and appraising as the returning moonlight more clearly revealed her to him. His gaze raked her from the mass of chestnut hair tumbling about her shoulders to the shapely legs below her buckskin breeches.

"Tell me, fair lady, do your, ah, clients have peculiar tastes, or are they merely so mean in the purse that they will not pay for a carriage. Place yourself under my protection, and I will be happy to provide for you in style.''

Arabella gasped and stared at him. ''Surely,'' she stammered, blushing furiously, ''you cannot think that I am a cyprian.''

''No, certainly I do not,'' he said coolly. ''They are above careening about the countryside in such a manner. I suspect your status is several steps lower.''

She gasped again, all her goodwill toward him crumbling. ''You are quite mistaken, sir.''

He grinned insolently at her indignation. ''Will next you tell me that you are a gently born lady of quality with faultless bloodlines?''

Stung, she protested, ''But I am!''

He laughed and cocked his eyebrow in mocking skepticism. ''Your illustrious name, milady?''

She visibly recoiled at the thought of giving it. She sought to conceal her discomfort by imitating, not very successfully, his calm. ''I am persuaded, sir, that given the unusual circumstances of this meeting, you will understand why I cannot reveal my identity to you.'' She tried to inject a note of dignity into her voice. ''As you can see, I am traveling incognito.''

He gave a shout of derisive laughter. ''I have never before seen a lady so eager to be incognito and to escape all notice that she adopts such a bizarre, attention-gathering costume.''

Arabella blushed furiously, knowing that she deserved this ridicule. She herself was now as curious about his identity as he was about hers. He had the appearance, manner, and speech of an aristocrat, yet she had never seen him among the ton. He had been at none of the many dinners, parties, and balls that she had attended in London, for she would not have forgotten such a handsome man.

With growing trepidation, she asked, ''Who are you?''

His dark eyes gleamed mischievously. ''Oh, no, I believe

in a name for a name," he told her, a hint of mocking laughter in his voice. "Only when you tell me yours shall I tell you mine."

She tossed her head haughtily. "I fear then, sir, that we shall have to remain anonymous to each other."

He shrugged indifferently. "Perhaps it is better that way." An insolent grin danced on his lips. "But I must have something from you to remember this night by."

Before Arabella realized what he was about, he took her in his arms and kissed her long and hard. So stunned was she by his sudden maneuver that she did not immediately try to break from his embrace. By the time she had recollected herself, his kiss had stirred in her something quite unlike anything she had ever before experienced. It seemed to sap both her strength and her will, making her a voluntary prisoner of his.

His kiss grew deeper and more intimate. It reluctantly penetrated Arabella's bemused senses how shockingly she was behaving. She struggled to free herself from him but found herself powerless in his strong arms. Twisting her head violently, she tried to escape those devilish lips, but he was too strong for her. She grew frantic, not from fear of his strength but fear of her weakness. If he continued to kiss her like this, she would soon lose any desire for him to stop.

Finally he let go, holding her at arm's length and grinning down at her with impudent eyes.

Arabella, who was as furious at herself for her weakness as she was at him for his audacity, said bitterly, "I thought you were my rescuer. How wrong it appears I was."

The grin widened, and he cocked a triangular eyebrow mockingly. "Are you going to swoon?"

She glared into his taunting eyes. "Of course not! I am not so silly as that."

"But any lady of quality would most certainly do so if she were so kissed," he mocked.

"You are outrageous!"

"And what of you? Will you deny how much you enjoyed my kiss."

Her face flamed with embarrassment, but her chin rose haughtily and she replied defiantly, "No, I will not. I have never been kissed like that before, and it was quite . . . quite . . . diverting."

He laughed. "At least you are honest—sometimes. But no woman of propriety would behave in such a disgraceful manner as you are tonight. Do you go for midnight rides often?"

Arabella blushed at the scorn in his voice and hung her head in shame. She knew that she deserved his disgust. Her incurable honesty would not permit her to make excuses to him. She swallowed hard and admitted in a tiny stricken voice, "You are quite right, of course. My conduct tonight richly deserves your harshest censure. I have given you no reason to think that I am a proper—"

"And every reason to think you are not," he interrupted. The dark eyes were no longer mocking but puzzled. "If you are what you say you are, why in God's name are you pulling such a crackbrained stunt as this—one guaranteed to put you beyond the pale of polite society?"

His scrutiny of her was now so intense that she faltered as she answered. "I am on an errand of the utmost urgency. I believe it to be perhaps even a matter of life and death." Tears formed in her eyes as she thought of Beth and her delicate health.

"Indeed I should hope it must be for you to risk your life, your virtue, and your reputation to ride in male garb, alone and unguarded at midnight." The harshness faded from his voice. "Surely you must be aware that this is one of the most notoriously dangerous pieces of ground in all England?"

She nodded. "I assure you that I would never have attempted it had there been any other way."

"Was your errand successful?"

The question brought an unhappy frown to her face, and her shoulders sagged. "I am afraid I have not yet carried it out." Her voice, too, was deflated. "I was riding to see him when . . ." She broke off, tears trickling down her cheeks.

"You must love him very much to risk so much for him," her companion said softly.

Her startled eyes flew up to his. "Oh, no, it is not I who love him but my sister."

"Your sister!" It was his turn to be startled. "You had better explain to me what you are about." He gave her an odd little smile. "Perhaps you might even be able to persuade me to help you."

"Would you?" she asked, hope flaring in her eyes.

"It depends on how moved I am by your story."

She told him about Beth, Justin, her stepmother, and Rufus Dobbs, although she was careful to omit all names.

When she finished, he said sharply, "Your scheme was madness."

Arabella, ever truthful, agreed. "Yes, it was. I see that now. But I was desperate. It was the only way I could think of getting a message to the lieutenant when there was no time. His regiment leaves at dawn."

The stranger asked wonderingly, "Do you love your sister so much that you would court lifelong disgrace and social ostracism?"

Arabella nodded.

"She is very fortunate to have a sister such as you."

"Oh, no, it is I who am fortunate to have her. If only you knew her, you would understand. Beth is the dearest, sweetest, gentlest creature."

The stranger was studying Arabella intently again. "So her name is Beth."

Arabella's hand flew to her mouth. "Oh," she gasped, much disconcerted. She nervously tried to reassure herself that she had not made a fatal slip. England was full of Beths.

She looked beseechingly up into his eyes. "Please will you help me now?"

He smiled down at her from his superior height. "Perhaps, since you have gone so far in this shatterbrained scheme." His face hardened. "But I shall help you only on one condition."

"What is it?" she faltered, fearful of what he would demand.

"That you will give me your solemn oath that you will never again indulge in such idiocy, that you will never again don men's clothes and ride across such dangerous ground as this either at night or alone."

"That is very easy for me to swear to," she told him frankly. "After what has happened tonight, be assured that I shall never embark on such a scheme again."

He smiled rather bleakly at her. "Learned your lesson, did you?"

She nodded, her eyes meeting his squarely. "Will you help me?"

"Yes, I will take you to the lieutenant, and then I will escort you back to London and your father's house in Arlington Street, Miss Arabella Vaughn."

She winced as though he had struck her. "How did you know my name?" she stammered when at last she found her tongue.

His dark eyes twinkled. "I didn't for certain until this moment when you confirmed it for me. I only suspected it before."

"What a wretched trick to play on me," she complained indignantly. "How could you suspect who I am? I am certain that we have never laid eyes on each other before tonight, for I should have remembered such . . ." She broke off, blushing scarlet at what her unruly tongue had been about to say.

"Such a fine figure as myself?" The terrible bitterness in his voice puzzled Arabella.

"We have seen each other before, but you were quite small, so you would hardly remember me."

"Nor should I think you would recognize me now."

"You are very like your mama," the stranger said.

"But I am not. I do not look at all like her. She was a great beauty."

Her reply amused him, relaxing the harsh set of his face. "And you think you are not beautiful?"

"No, indeed I am not. Beth is the beauty of the family. She looks just like mama."

"You may not look much like your mama, although you do have her charming dimples, but you are very much like her in spirit and forthrightness." He studied her face closely in the moonlight. "Your eyes are like hers, too, glowing with high spirits. And you tilt your head in the same manner that she did."

Arabella was dumbstruck by how well he seemed to have known her mama. She wracked her memory for some clue to his identity but could come up with nothing. In a mystified tone, she said, "You know so much about me and my family; please tell me who you are."

A mischievous smile played on his lips, making him look much younger and less austere. "I said I would tell you my name only if you would tell me yours. You refused, and so I refuse to tell you mine."

"But that's most unfair, when you know mine."

"Not, however, because you told it to me. You had your chance to learn mine and forfeited it. So I shall remain as anonymous to you, Miss Vaughn, as you had hoped to remain to me."

"But what am I to call you," she protested, "the midnight stranger?"

"Call me whatever you wish," he said indifferently. "It is getting very late. If we are to see Beth's lieutenant, we must be on our way immediately. Wait here while I bring the horses. I'll ride one of the bandits' back to where I left my own mount.''

As he moved away, Arabella asked, ''What shall we do with the highwaymen?''

''What can we do? Beth's lieutenant would not be pleased to have you turn up on his doorstep with such baggage.''

''But shouldn't we bury them?''

''Much as I would like to oblige you, Miss Vaughn, I rarely travel with a shovel.''

''How thoughtless of you!'' Arabella retorted.

As her benefactor collected Gray Charger and Bart's horse, she asked, ''How did you happen upon me?''

''I hardly happened upon you,'' he replied as they mounted. ''Your presence was well announced by the shots that were fired at you and by your screams.'' He pointed at the row of bog myrtle. ''I was by these when the commotion began, and I thought it prudent to conceal my horse and myself in them. I was fortunate enough to do so before Squint rode up and hid himself at the opposite end of the row. When you were halted, I made my way on foot to you.''

They had reached the stranger's horse, a lively bay, so well hidden among the shrubbery that they were almost upon it before Arabella saw it. A riding coat lay over the saddle, and the stranger donned it, explaining, ''I removed it in the interest of more silent movement.'' Mounting his own horse, he said, ''The road is this way.''

Arabella followed him. ''Where were you going tonight that you were on the heath?''

''Nowhere. I was merely out for a ride.''

''On Hounslow Heath?'' she exclaimed in disbelief. ''At such an hour?''

''Unfortunate circumstances have confined me indoors of late. Tonight I found I could escape for a few hours. I ached for a fast gallop, which is impossible in the city, so I came here.''

Arabella shuddered at what her fate might have been had he not made that decision.

"Now," he said briskly before she could question him further, "we must discuss what we shall do when we reach our destination."

"Go immediately to the lieutenant's quarters."

"We shall do nothing of the sort," he told her in a tone that brooked no argument. "If you hope to preserve a shred of reputation you dare not march into the quarters of bachelor officers under any circumstances and most certainly not dressed like that. Someone is bound to recognize you. I shall bring the lieutenant to you."

"He may not go with a stranger."

The question stopped her benefactor for a moment, then he said, "I will tell him that I am a neighbor of yours at Lindley Park."

Arabella blinked in surprise at his mention of the Vaughns' country house in Kent. "What name will you give Justin?"

He paused again. "Ah, Mr. Smith. Mr. Howard Smith."

"Is that your name?"

He grinned. "Of course not, but the lieutenant will not know that. Now let me tell you exactly what we shall do. You will remain well out of sight while I find a respectable inn where I can hire a private parlor. Once I have done that, I will contrive to smuggle you into it unseen. You will wait there while I find the lieutenant and bring him to you."

He stared thoughtfully at her in the moonlight. "I hope for Beth's sake that you are as persuasive with her lieutenant as you have been with me!"

Chapter 4

❧

Arabella and the midnight stranger heard the army encampment long before they reached its village. Raucous shouts, curses, and laughter rent the quiet of the night. The soldiers were celebrating in drunken revelry their last hours in the camp and their uncertain future.

On the outskirts of the village, the two riders passed a cottage where clothes had been left to air upon a line. "Stop a moment here," Arabella's companion said, reining in his horse.

He dismounted and, pulling a large roll of money from his pocket, peeled off a five-pound note. He went to the line, where he removed a plaid calico skirt and pinned in its place the banknote. Returning to her side, he folded the garment neatly.

"Whatever are you doing, Mr. Smith?" Arabella asked, deciding that although it was not his real name, it was better than none at all.

"I am persuaded that if the good lieutenant sees his beloved's outrageous sister dressed in men's breeches, he might have misgivings about his own darling." Mr. Smith's tone was teasing, but his dark eyes were serious.

"Oh, but Beth is not at all like me," Arabella assured him. "She would never dream of doing such a thing."

"How fortunate for her and her longevity," he observed dryly, "not to mention her lieutenant's peace of mind."

"Yes, isn't it! I assure you that she is not at all outrageous like me."

"How boring."

Arabella giggled. "Not at all. You would adore Beth. Everyone does."

He handed her the folded skirt. "Conceal this beneath your coat." He swung back up into his saddle.

Arabella looked down at the cheap calico garment in her hand. "I do not think that you received fair exchange," she teased. "Five pounds would purchase ten skirts of this quality."

"I was paying a premium for its accessibility. I am persuaded that on you, however, it will look worth ten times what I gave for it." His dark eyes swept her admiringly.

Arabella, who thought herself immune to compliments, was strangely thrilled by his.

As they cantered down the main street of the village, Arabella was shocked by the scene unfolding ahead of her. Soldiers and camp followers, many with tankards still in hand, had overflowed the taverns into the streets, where bonfires had been set casting an eerie glow over the forms of those men who had already drunk themselves into oblivion and lay passed-out on the road.

Others were singing drunkenly at a tuneless volume that made Arabella's ears ache. Still others entertained themselves by grabbing at whatever woman was in sight. The women, in low-cut, gaudy gowns, returned the embraces indiscriminately and were as drunk as their companions. Arabella was aghast. Never in her sheltered life had she seen such shocking behavior.

The townsfolk, except for one unfortunate lad on horseback, had abandoned the streets to the soldiers and their camp followers and locked themselves safely indoors for the night. The youth, trying to make his way down the teeming street, was harassed by soldiers who jibed and cursed at him and tried to pull him from the saddle. Finally they succeeded. He was dumped unceremoniously in the street, where the drunken crowd surrounded him.

"We shall turn here," Mr. Smith said, leading Arabella down a silent side street away from the pandemonium. "This way is longer, but there will be no curious eyes to penetrate your disguise."

Arabella shivered. How thankful she was for her companion. Had she tried to ride down that street alone, she most likely would have fared even worse than the poor lad. She was struck again by her enormous folly in undertaking her errand. How hopeless it would have been to have found Justin and met secretly with him. She shivered again at the thought of what would have happened to her had the midnight stranger not rescued her.

He seemed to have the same thought, for he frowned and said savagely, "Why the devil did your brother not ride to see the lieutenant instead of you?"

Arabella hastened to defend her twin. "Brom does not know what happened. He never comes home when Papa is gone from London as he is now. Brom and my stepmother do not get along."

"When did your papa remarry?" the stranger asked.

"A year ago."

In the moonlight, she saw a startled look flit across his face. "But your mama has been dead only a year and a half. Who is your stepmother?"

"The daughter of the curate in the village near Lindley Park."

"Good Lord, not Fanny Igles!"

Arabella exclaimed, "You know her!"

"We have never been introduced, but I have heard a good deal about her."

"From whom?"

"Friends," he replied evasively.

"I wish that Papa might have talked to your friends before he married her," Arabella said sadly. "How much happier our lives would have been."

"From what I heard of her, Fanny always was determined to marry above herself, and at last she succeeded," he mused. "But whatever possessed your father to shackle himself to that dreadful woman, especially after your exquisite mama."

Arabella colored and squirmed in the saddle.

Her obvious discomfort brought a sardonic quirk to Mr. Smith's lips. "So the determined Fanny arranged a trap! Did she see to it that she and your father were found together in a compromising position?"

"How did you guess?" Arabella cried.

"She had tried such tactics unsuccessfully before."

"On whom?"

"I cannot tell. I am very discreet. Why do she and your brother not get along?"

"She particularly dislikes him, I think because she hopes to have a son who would inherit Papa's title and estate, and Brom stands in the way of that. She rips at him constantly. He can do nothing right in her eyes, and he has long since given up trying. She has transformed him into a sullen rebel." Arabella's face clouded with worry at the thought of what Lady Elizabeth had told her, and she blurted out, "I am so worried about him! He has fallen into the clutches of a scheming female and wants to marry her."

"Who is this female?"

"She told Brom her name is Julie Berner, but my cousin Lance insists that she is actually a notorious young demirep named Julia Coates."

"Julia Coates! But she is living under the protection of—" Mr. Smith broke off, looking troubled.

"Do you know her?" Arabella cried, much shocked.

"I am well acquainted with many ladies of the demi-monde." Seeing Arabella's stricken face in the moonlight, he said carelessly, "Don't look so horrified. I am not a saint. In fact, most people would say that I am much more likely related to the devil."

Her eyes widened. "Surely you are not disreputable?"

"Excessively so," he assured her. "As for Brom, who is eighteen and hasn't a feather to fly with, he will be quite safe from Julia Coates. He is not at all what she requires."

"But I am told that she deliberately ensnared him."

"That makes no sense," he said flatly. "Why is your brother not a student, instead of racking around London's lowlife?"

"He was sent down from Oxford."

"A slow top?"

"No, but he is not at all bookish. He loves riding, shooting, hunting, fishing, and mechanical things. He is not a bad boy," Arabella added defensively.

"Only badly handled?"

Arabella nodded, pleased again by her companion's quick understanding. "If only Papa would have paid some attention to him over the years. He never did the things fathers are supposed to do with sons, never taught him to ride or shoot or hunt. Mama tried to make up for Papa's neglect. When she died, poor Brom was even more distraught than the rest of us."

"And your papa remarried so quickly."

Arabella nodded. "Brom resented that. Then Lady Vaughn has been so wretched to him. He has grown increasingly rebellious and unmanageable."

Arabella and her companion came to a quiet inn. She waited in the shadows of the courtyard while he secured a private parlor for her. After the proprietor returned to the bed from which he had been roused, Mr. Smith smuggled her inside. The parlor was small and plainly furnished, but clean and adequate.

"When I return," the stranger said, preparing to set off in search of Justin, "I shall give three short raps on the door. Do not open it to any other knock." His brown eyes, soft as velvet, were very serious. "I do not think you will be disturbed, but I beg of you to take no chances."

In the lamplight, his face was even more handsome than it had seemed in the moonlight. His skin was not naturally dark but deeply tanned. The lamplight revealed, too, tiny lines about the eyes and mouth that told Arabella that her earlier guess about his age had most likely been correct.

As he opened the door to go, she suddenly felt lost and frightened at his leaving her.

His sharp eyes caught her tremor, and he demanded, "What is it?"

"What . . . what if you do not return?"

His smile was so reassuring that it seemed to warm her to her toes. "But of course I shall return—and with Justin. Have no fear of that."

After he shut the door behind him, she hurried to a small mirror hanging above a washstand that had a porcelain bowl and ewer of tepid water upon it. She was shocked by her disheveled appearance. Her face was smudged, long wisps of chestnut hair had strayed from beneath Brom's hat, and his riding coat was dirty where she had fallen upon it when she had been yanked from her horse by the highwayman.

Tossing aside the hat and riding coat, she hastily washed herself, then combed and redid her hair into neat coils. She changed from the buckskin breeches into the calico skirt.

Although it was a little large for her slender figure, it fortunately hung to the floor, concealing her hessian boots.

She checked herself in the mirror. Although her costume

was plain, she looked neat and respectable. Justin would not be shocked when he saw her.

If he saw her.

Another half hour passed, and her despair grew with each passing minute. At last, she heard footsteps in the hall outside, followed by three quick raps on the door. She hastened to open it.

Justin stood there with Mr. Smith.

Arabella could have wept with relief, even though the lieutenant's normally open, friendly face was disapproving and his eyes smoldering.

"Arabella," he said coldly, "I could not believe this man when he insisted that you were here and must see me. What madness is this?"

Arabella's heart sank.

Mr. Smith said sternly, "I have told you, Lieutenant Keats, that Miss Vaughn has risked much to come to you tonight. I hope you are worthy of her sacrifice."

Justin's frown dissipated into confusion. Arabella shot Mr. Smith a grateful look. *What a hopeless disaster this night would have been without him.*

He stepped into the hall, shutting the door so that Arabella and Justin might talk in private.

"Justin," Arabella cried, "everything that Lady Vaughn told you today was a lie. Beth adores you. That is why I had to come. Poor Beth would die if she thought that you left for war thinking her untrue to you."

Hope glowed in the bleak embers that were Justin Keats's eyes.

Arabella told him of Lady Vaughn's mendacity, of Beth's reaction to Justin's letter, and of her sister's heartbreak when she learned why he had written it.

"I was persuaded that if I did not come to you tonight, Beth would go into a fatal decline," Arabella concluded. "She would not live to see your return."

"If I returned," Justin said bitterly. "When I left your house today, I looked forward to a quick death in battle to end my misery."

"You need never doubt Beth's love for you. It burns as bright as the sun at noon. Please, I beg of you, write her a few lines now, reassuring her that you love her, too, and that this terrible misunderstanding is cleared away."

Justin did as he was bid, sitting down at a small writing table in the corner of the parlor. Finding paper in its drawer, he spent several minutes covering three pages with his large, firm writing.

As he handed the completed note to Arabella, he asked, "Why would your stepmother act in such a despicable manner?"

"Lady Vaughn hopes to recoup the family fortunes by extracting a large price for Beth's hand."

Seeing his puzzled look, Arabella told him frankly of her father's dire financial circumstances.

To her surprise, Justin paled and stammered, "Will Beth have no portion?"

Arabella was shocked. "But you will have each other," she reminded him. "Is that not enough for you?"

"For me, yes," Justin said in an agonized tone, "but I am the sole support of my mother and three unmarried sisters. I send them every penny I can, but it is not enough, and they subsist in such poverty that it breaks my heart. Yet I have nothing more to give them. I would not dream of condemning Beth to such a life. I love her too much. And she deserves so much better."

She does, Arabella thought, unable to hide her dismay.

Justin looked at Arabella with misery and shame in his eyes. "Please understand that I am not mercenary, but I was counting on Beth's portion as the foundation on which I could eventually build a comfortable life for us. I despise the army. I never wanted to join, but it was the only avenue that my family would permit one of its impoverished twigs to take. I had hoped that with Beth's portion I could sell out and buy us a country property large enough to support us as well as my mother and sisters. But now I will not even be able to do that. Oh, Arabella, what am I to do?''

She could not answer his agonized question.

"There must be a way," Justin cried in despair, "but I am at a loss to know what it can be."

So was Arabella.

Chapter 5

The financial barriers to Beth and Justin's marrying seemed so insurmountable to Arabella that she was uncharacteristically quiet as she and the stranger set out to return to London. She had discarded the calico skirt for the buckskin breeches and tucked her hair beneath Brom's hat. Once again she had arranged the heavy scarf about her neck to conceal the lower portion of her face. Cantering along on their mounts, Arabella and her companion appeared to be two men traveling late.

As they rode out of the village, they avoided the main street, from which the sounds of drunken revelry still rang out. When they reached the cottage on the village outskirts where Mr. Smith had borrowed the calico skirt, he stopped, dismounted, and replaced the skirt on the line, carefully pinning the five-pound note to it.

As he remounted his big bay, Arabella asked, "Since you returned the skirt, why did you leave the money?"

He shrugged his broad shoulders. "Rental for its use. From the look of the clothes, their owner needs the blunt far more than I do."

How good and generous her benefactor was, Arabella thought as they rode on.

They traveled another mile in silence. The sounds of the

partying soldiers slowly faded away. No other riders were upon the road.

Finally Mr. Smith observed, "You seem quite blue-deviled, Miss Vaughn. Were you not able to convince the lieutenant of your sister's love for him?"

Arabella loosened the uncomfortable scarf and pulled it away from her lower face. "Justin believed me. I carry a letter from him to Beth, but . . ." She swallowed hard.

"But what?" the stranger prompted gently.

There was so much kindness and sympathy in his tone that Arabella found herself telling him about Justin's poverty and heavy responsibilities.

She concluded by saying, "I did not tell Justin, nor will I say anything to Beth, but I cannot see how they will ever be able to marry. Even if my stepmother fails in her scheme to marry my sister to Rufus Dobbs for a large sum, Papa would never permit Beth to marry into such poverty."

"Rufus Dobbs is the suitor that you told me about!" her companion exclaimed in disbelief. "Surely your papa would never allow such a man to marry Beth no matter how much money he offered."

"I hope you are right," Arabella said wistfully, "but I fear Papa may be on the brink of debtors' prison, and if it comes to that, he might—" She broke off, flushing.

"Be desperate enough to sacrifice Beth?" her companion finished for her.

She nodded reluctantly and tried to explain. "Papa is very indolent. He has never been much interested in his children, and he likes his comfort above all else."

"Debtors' prison would be most uncomfortable," Mr. Smith agreed dryly. "How did your papa get into such financial straits? I thought him well fixed. Lindley Park is a fine estate and should be quite profitable."

"It should be," Arabella replied, again surprised at how much he seemed to know about her family. "But Papa has never been good at managing either his finances or his lands. Mama, when she was alive, had to take over running the estate as well as the household. She managed both with great economy."

"But after she died, your papa's careless management undid him?"

"Partly, but mostly it is Lady Vaughn's excessive extravagance. She spends more in a month than Mama did in three years."

"Why do you always refer to her so formally—as Lady Vaughn?"

"She expressly ordered that we should do so. She would not hear of our calling her Mama. She said it would look quite foolish, when she is so nearly our own age."

"So nearly! But she must be nine years older than you."

"She is. I think her real reason is that she so loves being addressed as Lady."

The night was warm and still. The storm clouds that had covered the sky earlier had vanished, leaving Arabella and her companion illuminated by the silver three-quarter moon and millions of bright stars. How much less menacing the night seemed to her now. She knew, however, that the credit did not belong to the moonlight but to the powerfully built man riding beside her.

"How do you like London?" he asked.

"I don't," she confessed.

He looked startled. "Why not?"

"It's boring."

"London *boring*! Surely you jest."

"Not the city itself," Arabella conceded, "but the life I lead there. It is so excessively idle. We do nothing but make calls and go to parties, where we see all the same people and hear all the same stories over and over. I must change my gown a half dozen times a day, and—"

"But think of all the beautiful gowns you get to wear that way," he teased.

"They are beautiful to look at, but not to wear when they must be laced as tightly as Lady Vaughn insists upon."

He grinned at Arabella. "I wager you find being a demure young lady of quality a dead bore and wish you had been born a boy, don't you?"

She nodded with sparkling eyes. Never in her life had she met a man who seemed to understand her so well and whose company she so enjoyed. "How I long for the freedom to put aside my stays and ride in clothes such as this across the countryside!"

They reached Hounslow Heath. Although it did not seem so frightening with Mr. Smith's formidable figure at her side, Arabella could not entirely quiet her apprehension that a highwayman might be concealed behind one of the bog myrtle bushes, which stood as tall as a man, and would lunge out at her and her companion as they rode by.

He looked at her with dark eyes that were serious and searching in the moonlight. "I suspect that your stepmother strives to make your life as miserable as she does your brother's."

Once again Arabella was impressed by his quick comprehension of unspoken undercurrents. "Lady Vaughn finds my hoydenish behavior and frank tongue shocking."

"And undoubtedly she is quick to point out every one of your lapses from her standards."

"At length," Arabella admitted. "Lady Vaughn says that I am totally lacking in the feminine wiles necessary to capture a husband."

"Thank God you are lacking in her kind of wiles," her companion said fervently.

Arabella thought that her stepmother's blighting company was a major reason why London was so disappointing. She sighed. "If only I could go home to Lindley Park and leave Lady Vaughn in London."

"But think how disappointed all your suitors would be if you deserted London," Mr. Smith teased.

"I have very few suitors—at least very few who are both serious and eligible."

"I cannot believe that you do not have dozens of both eligible and serious suitors."

Arabella's honesty required her to assure him, "Oh, but I am not at all the crack. You see, I have the odious habit of always saying what I think."

"Oh that *is* very bad ton indeed," he agreed gravely.

"Yes it is, and worse," she continued tragically, "I cannot ever manage to act coy and demure."

He cocked a triangular black eyebrow. "In short, you are not insipid."

"How nice you are to say so!"

A smile tugged at the corners of her companion's mouth. "What makes a suitor eligible?"

"Birth and breeding. He must be of distinguished family."

"Of course you would never think of marrying an ineligible suitor."

Mr. Smith's tone was teasing, but Arabella's reply was quite serious. "No, that would never do."

"I should think an ineligible suitor would appeal to your romantic soul," he teased.

"I am not at all romantic."

He grinned. "I am surprised that a girl as unconventional as you would never consider an ineligible suitor."

"I am not at all unconventional when it comes to marriage. I know my duty to my family." Noticing that a frown had settled on his face, Arabella said defensively, "I daresay you think that I am excessively proud of my lineage, but it has been stressed to me as long as I can remember."

Seeing his frown deepen, Arabella felt compelled to explain herself further. "To marry unsuitably would mean becoming a social outcast, and I could not bear that. Harriet Mobley, the daughter of a squire in the neighborhood, eloped to Gretna Green with the son of a village tradesman. They were wildly in love with each other, and he is an honest, industrious young man who makes her a fine husband. But she is cut by everyone. Her parents refuse to even see her baby or acknowledge him as their grandchild."

"Is she cut by you, too?"

"Lady Vaughn forbade me to speak to her, but occasionally I manage to sneak off to see her. I am the only one who ever does so, and she is so terribly lonely. It is just like it was for poor Aunt Nell."

Arabella's face clouded at the memory of that dazzling, charismatic woman, who had not actually been her aunt, although her mama and Nell had been closer than even sisters.

"Nell Fitzhugh was the most marvelous, charming creature I can ever remember meeting," Arabella explained. "But she was ostracized because she was the earl of Woodthorpe's mistress."

The stranger's face turned forbidding, and Arabella hastened to defend Nell from his condemnation. "Oh, I know people tell the most wicked stories about her, but most of them are untrue. They say she was a serving wench, but in fact, she was the daughter of an old Irish family. They say she was a light-skirt, but my mama said the earl was the only man in Nell's life. When they eloped to Gretna Green, his father caught them, dragged him away, and forced him to marry another woman. After that, her relatives would have nothing to do with her."

Arabella paused and stole a glance at her companion's face. It remained set in harshly angry lines. Arabella sighed. Poor Nell. Everyone condemned that enchanting woman.

"If only I could make people understand what a wonderful

creature she was," Arabella cried. "I was a very little girl when she died, but I still remember her so vividly. She lived at Willow Wood, which adjoins our own Lindley Park. She was ostracized by everyone but my mama, who loved her. No one else spoke to her. Even her servants had to be hired from London, because none of the local people would work for her." Arabella shook her head sadly. "I could not bear such an existence, cut off from all my friends, relatives, and neighbors."

Still the stranger said nothing, but his frown had deepened almost to a scowl.

They rode in silence between miniature hills of heather, the sound of their horses' hooves dulled by the marshy ground. Arabella noticed that Mr. Smith's eyes were ever vigilant, constantly studying the landscape.

Never had she so enjoyed a man. His strength and courage had won her admiration; his humor, understanding, and obvious breeding had won her trust—and more. She remembered his kiss. To her chagrin, she longed to feel his lips upon hers again.

"Are you married?" Arabella asked. The question surprised her quite as much as it did him.

"Why do you ask?"

She was not entirely certain of the answer herself. To cover her confusion, she stammered, "I—I thought I might call upon your wife."

This prospect seemed to amuse him greatly. "And tell her what? That you met her husband as you were fighting off highwaymen on one of your solitary rides on Hounslow Heath?"

His answer stabbed her with pain. So he did have a wife! "Your wife would be terribly shocked by my behavior, wouldn't she?"

"Undoubtedly," he said sternly. "If I had one, but I don't."

Arabella suddenly was very happy. "Why don't you?"

"Why don't I what? Have a wife?"

She nodded.

"Is there nothing you won't ask?" he said in a voice trembling with laughter.

"But you haven't answered my question," Arabella persisted.

"I have never met a woman that I wanted to be shackled to."

"Do you dislike women?" she asked, suddenly alarmed.

He laughed, a rich, musical laugh. "To the contrary, I like women—in the plural—too well."

"Are you a loose screw?" Arabella blurted.

Her benefactor demanded wrathfully, "Do you know what that means?"

"No, not exactly," Arabella admitted. "But I do not believe it is very nice."

"You are right on that score," he said in a choking voice.

When they reached the outskirts of London, Mr. Smith asked, "Didn't your father wound Lord Whittleson years ago in a duel?"

"Yes," Arabella replied, puzzled by the question. "Whittleson was one of Mama's suitors. In fact, my grandfather, the duke of Lysted, favored him, but then Papa made his offer; and Mama accepted him. Whittleson called Papa out."

It was hard for Arabella to conceive of her indolent father bestirring himself to fight a duel, but then he would have done anything for her mama. Besides, Whittleson had left Lord Vaughn no choice.

"Wasn't there some scandal attached to that duel?" Mr. Smith asked.

Arabella nodded. "Whittleson cheated and fired before the count was finished, but he missed. Papa deliberately gave him only a slight wound. Of course, such conduct made Papa a hero and Whittleson a villain. Whittleson should have been grateful that Papa did not kill him, but instead he told Papa that it was too bad that he hadn't because he would live to rue not having done so. But nothing ever came of his threat. Why do you ask?''

Mr. Smith shrugged. ''Idle curiosity.''

The streets of London were deserted and more silent than Arabella, who hated the din of the city, would have believed possible. Only an occasional Charlie, standing watch in his sentry box, was awake to witness the passage of two riders, one on a big bay and the other on a gray.

Soon they would be in Arlington Street, and still Arabella had no clue to her benefactor's identity. He had been so kind and sympathetic and understanding. Never before had she been able to talk so freely of her concerns to anyone as she had been to this stranger. Not even to Sally Cromwell, who was her closest friend, or to her sister, Beth, who was too easily upset.

Arabella again pressed him for his name, but he adamantly refused to reveal it. ''No, a bargain is a bargain, and I always demand strict adherence to any that I make.''

''But I shall always wonder who you are,'' she protested.

''Will you?'' he asked in a tone that seemed strangely sad.

''Surely we shall meet at some ball or assembly.''

''We won't,'' he said curtly. ''We do not travel in the same circles.''

Her heart ached at his indifference to seeing her again. ''You appear to be a gentleman of the first water.''

''Appearances can be deceiving. I told you I am excessively disreputable.''

''What did you do?''

''Nothing.'' The bitterness in that one word was so profound that Arabella stared at him. His aristocratic face had tightened into a cold, hard mask. ''Nothing at all.''

"I do not understand," she faltered.

"We are almost at your father's house," he said brus-
quely. "How do we get into the stable?"

She directed him. Once inside, he insisted upon taking care
of Gray Charger for her. He told her to go at once to her room,
but she refused, saying that she would not chance his being
discovered alone in the stable and mistaken for a horse thief.
But that was not her real reason for staying. She could not
bring herself to leave him, not knowing who he was or
whether she would ever see him again.

As he removed the gelding's saddle, a disquieting
thought struck Arabella. If he was as disreputable as he
said, would he tell about her escapade tonight? Hot color
rushed to her cheeks. "You—you won't say anything about
what happened tonight—about me?" she stammered, her
eyes pleading.

"Of course not." He was clearly irritated that she had
thought it was necessary to ask. "If ever we should meet
again, I promise you that I shall not give the slightest sign that
I have met you before."

If ever we should meet again. The words filled Arabella
with a dismay bordering on despair.

As he finished with Gray Charger, he smiled gently at her.
"Remember your promise to me that you will never again do
anything so foolish as what you did tonight."

She nodded, a lump rising in her throat. "I can never thank
you enough for all that you did for me."

He stared down at her, his eyes so soft that she was reminded again of rich brown velvet. His head inclined toward
hers. For a moment she thought he meant to kiss her again.
Her heart, usually so imperturbably quiet and steady, was
suddenly thumping like a drum. Mesmerized by his close-
ness and by the memory of his earlier kiss, her eyelids half
closed; and she waited for his lips to find hers.

But he drew back suddenly and hurried from the stable without kissing her, without even a farewell.

Arabella stared after him, stunned by how sharp her disappointment was that he had not kissed her.

Chapter 6

෯

Once inside the house, Arabella sneaked on tiptoe up the back stairs and along the hall to Brom's empty room. The candle she had left beside his bed had burned low in its brass holder but still sent out a flickering light. Hastily she shed his riding clothes and donned her night shift and dressing gown. She picked up the brass candlestick. With Justin's letter in her other hand, she crept down the hall to her own room.

At the sound of the door closing, Beth stirred restlessly. Arabella laid her cool hand on her sister's still-hot brow. Beth's eyes fluttered open, and she stared up at Arabella.

"Did, did Brom come?"

Arabella did not want to lie to Beth and instead evaded. "My dearest, it has all been taken care of. Justin knows the truth." Arabella thrust his letter into her sister's delicate, trembling hands. "Here, he has even sent a letter to you."

Beth came fully awake with a gasp and sat up to read it. As her eyes traveled down the handwritten page, her lovely face grew happier with each line. When she was done, she threw her arms tightly around Arabella and cried ecstatically, "All is right again between Justin and me!"

Arabella forced a smile to her lips. "I am so happy for you." She could not destroy her sister's joy by telling her that

Justin's poverty would surely make their marriage impossible. Instead, Arabella's fertile mind sought some way to bring about their union.

Beth sighed and laid her head back on the pillow. "How good you and Brom are to me. If only I could pay you both back for what you have done for me tonight."

Panicked that Beth would say something to their brother, Arabella said hastily, "You can repay us both by never mentioning it again. It would be dreadful if somehow Lady Vaughn were to find out. You know how she hates Brom already. Please promise me you will never speak of it."

Beth's face was puzzled. "If you insist," she began slowly.

Arabella squeezed her hand. "I insist. It is the least you can do for Brom."

Despite Arabella's exhaustion, once her head was upon the pillow she could not sleep. Her mind was in a turmoil. She could see only one possible hope for Beth and Justin: If Arabella wed Lord Estes, perhaps she could convince him to help the unlucky lovers. Yet the thought of marrying Lord Estes, which only a few hours earlier had seemed so appealing to Arabella, now depressed her. She could not drive from her mind a pair of brown eyes like soft velvet and a kiss that promised a new and unexplored world of pleasure that she had never even suspected existed. Never had Lord Estes aroused such agitation within her.

Then she remembered the stranger's cool words, "*If ever we should meet again.*" His indifference to seeing her again rankled cruelly. She told herself resolutely that she could not afford to throw away a brilliant match for the ethereal dream of a mysterious stranger who by his own admission was most disreputable. She must wed Lord Estes—and then persuade him to help Beth and Justin financially.

Arabella and Lady Vaughn attended a rout that night at the

marquess of Tonbridge's. Beth stayed home, pleading that she did not yet feel well enough to go. The assembly room was already packed with people when Arabella and her step-mother arrived.

Arabella eagerly scanned the crowd for a giant of a man with black hair, velvet brown eyes, and wide shoulders encased in an elegantly tailored coat. Even though the midnight stranger had told her that she would not see him among London society, she swallowed hard, trying to down her irrational disappointment that he was not there.

Listening to bits of conversation drifting around her, she discovered that everyone was talking of the deaths the previous night of the notorious highwaymen Big Bart and Squint Bailey on Hounslow Heath.

"Lord Alvanley says a fox went ahunting and caught himself two wolves," Arabella overheard Lord Rudolph Oldfield say. "What is odd is that the fox has not claimed the sizable reward."

Arabella strained to hear more of Oldfield's conversation, but Lord Estes appeared beside her and asked Lady Vaughn's permission to steal Arabella away. Her Ladyship was only too glad to agree to whatever Lord Estes might wish.

As always, his attire was splendidly showy. His blue-and-black striped silk coat was worn over a white silk waistcoat embroidered with dentelle and shades of silk. His black pantaloons had been molded to his corseted waist and hips. A huge sapphire, matching the blue stripe of his coat, sparkled from the silky folds of his intricately tied cravat. Equally intricate was the careful arrangement of blond curls about his face. Another large sapphire glittered on the finger of one of his manicured hands, and the buckles on his black pumps were edged in tiny sapphires.

As he made his way through the crowd with Arabella, a sneer played on his well-formed mouth. She saw it there frequently when he contemplated those around him. It was as

though His Lordship, secure in his great consequence as heir
to a fine title and an even finer fortune, found much of the
world and its inhabitants beneath his touch. Arabella, who
delighted in people no matter what their station in life, found
Estes's cold disdain unsettling.

He led her into the refreshment room, where a supper had
been laid out on long tables along one wall. Small tables with
chairs had been set about elsewhere in the room for the convenience of the diners. It was early, however, and the room
was empty except for servants.

Lord Estes ignored the food and led Arabella to a small
table with two chairs in the far corner. He held a chair for
Arabella, then moved the second very close to hers and sat
down. As he did so, she caught the odor of liquor upon his
breath.

A servant appeared immediately at their table with two
glasses of champagne on a tray. His Lordship snatched them,
gave one glass to Arabella, and took a long drink from the
other before setting it on the table before him. He said abruptly, without preamble, "Would it distress you if I were to
speak to your father about us—our future?"

Estes's condescending tone told Arabella that he was certain she would be delighted, not distressed. Her pride flared.
So certain was he of his own desirability, he could not conceive of any woman refusing him. For an instant she was
tempted to upset his certainty. But she remembered Beth and
Justin. Their happiness depended upon what Arabella did tonight. She dared not indulge her annoyance at their expense.
So instead she replied with uncharacteristic meekness. "I
should be very pleased." As she spoke, a pair of mocking
brown eyes rose up in her mind to brand her a liar. "However, I must warn you that I can bring you no portion."

Estes shrugged. "I have no need of it. As soon as my father dies, I shall be rich as Midas. I shall speak to your father
tomorrow."

Arabella's eyes had clouded at his mention of Wood-thorpe's approaching death. She remembered all too vividly her own anguish during her beloved mama's final days, and she said fervently, "I cannot tell you how saddened I am to hear of your father's illness. Is there no hope?"

Lord Estes grinned at her. "I pray to God not."

Arabella was so stunned that she very nearly dropped her glass of champagne in her lap. "What a dreadful thing to say," she blurted.

"Oh, do not sound so missish," he told her carelessly. "All the world knows my father and I cannot abide each other. Even now that he is dying, he refuses to see me, and I could not be happier about his ban. It spares me the ordeal of having to make hypocritical expressions of solicitude to him."

The coldness of Lord Estes's slate-blue eyes chilled Arabella. "But he is *your father,* and he is dying!" she cried, setting her glass down so hard upon the table that some of its pale contents splashed over the rim.

"You must understand that my father and I despise each other." Estes took a long drink of champagne. "Nor is he alone on his deathbed, although that is what he deserves. He has his bas—" Lord Estes, remembering the company he was in, caught himself and hastily amended, "his Irish by-blow to comfort him in his final hours."

Arabella's estimation of Lord Estes was undergoing a rapid and troubling transformation. "Why do you hate your father?"

He shrugged and took another long drink of champagne. "We never got along. We had a final falling-out recently."

"Over what?"

"He refused to pay more of my gambling debts unless I retired with him to the country, where I was to work off the monies he'd advanced me." Lord Estes's voice was laced with contempt. "He'd made Damon, his disgusting oaf by his Irish slut, a slavey, and he thought to do the same with me.'' Lord Estes tilted his head proudly. ''But I would have none of that. I am a Howard out of a Chatner, and I shall not lower myself to menial tasks so far below my consequence.''

''How were you to work your debts off?''

''I was to learn how to run estates and''—His Lordship twisted his voice into a satiric mockery of his father's—''learn the value of the money I was throwing away at the gaming tables.'' Lord Estes drained his champagne glass and snorted. ''The evil old reprobate. As if he didn't throw away enough money on his whores.''

Arabella was not unsympathetic to the earl's aim. If only someone had taught Papa such skills, perhaps the Vaughns would not be in quite such straits now. She asked gently, ''Is it menial to learn to manage your lands?''

''Most certainly.'' Lord Estes snatched another glass of champagne from the tray of a passing footman. ''No nobleman should soil his hands thus.''

''But your father did. It is said he increased his wealth manyfold by his wise management.''

''Which is one more reason in a long line why he is no gentleman.''

Lord Estes had never before discussed himself or his father with Arabella. Now she saw with sickening clarity that he was revealing his true nature, which he had hidden behind a reserved, well-mannered facade.

''How can you speak so about your own father?'' she demanded.

''To know him is to hate him.'' His Lordship drank heavily from his new glass of champagne.

An unhappy frown knitted Arabella's face. She had been very small when the earl had abandoned Willow Wood after the death of his beloved Nell, and Arabella had not remembered him as she had the marvelous Nell. To this day the neighborhood still talked of Woodthorpe and his by-blow as though they were the devil and his hell-born spawn.

It had, therefore, been a shock to Arabella when the earl had come to her mama's funeral and she had discovered that he was charming. Tall, broad, and still handsome in a dissipated sort of way, he had been shrewdly intelligent and witty. Having heard so much about what a wicked, dreadful man he was, she had had grave difficulty reconciling him with the evil picture that others had painted of him. It was no more true than the picture that was painted of Nell, whom she did remember.

"Why have you suddenly become so quiet?" Lord Estes asked.

Arabella said hastily, "Does your mother approve of our marriage?"

Estes nodded. "Yes, you come from an old and distinguished line, although there is that odious, vulgar stepmother of yours, whom I detest. But, of course, she is only your relation by marriage. Still, I cannot like any connection with her." He sniffed fastidiously. "My mother is coming to London to meet you."

"She is!" Arabella exclaimed in surprise. It was well known that the countess, who was said to be a dreadful shrew, had not come to London in years, preferring to remain ensconced at Woodthorpe Hall, the ancient Gothic monstrosity in Yorkshire that had been the lifelong country residence of every earl of Woodthorpe save the present one. He, early in his miserable marriage, had abandoned the hall to his wife.

Arabella said slowly, "If your father dies, we shall not be able to be married until after the mourning period is over."

"Nonsense. I wish to marry immediately, and my mother wishes it, too." Lord Estes emptied the bubbling contents of his glass. "We are both most anxious that I sire an heir as quickly as possible. We must make absolutely certain that scum Damon has no chance of inheriting anything." Estes's slate-blue eyes narrowed in hatred. "If I were to die without an heir, he might have a claim."

A cold shadow fell across Arabella's heart. Estes had uttered not a word about loving her or even having the least affection for her, only about the urgency of producing a son to keep his half brother from inheriting. Swallowing her pride, she asked in a small voice, "Do you love me?"

He shrugged carelessly. "I am making you an offer, aren't I? But do not expect flowery protestations from me. That is not at all my style."

Arabella, who had thought herself totally unromantic, discovered just how wrong she had been. Only the thought of Beth kept Arabella from telling Estes to take his offer and go to the devil. But she had to insure at least her sister's happiness. Arabella tried to console herself with the thought that once married, she could escape London and live at Woodthorpe Hall. Choking down her unhappiness, she asked, "Shall I like Woodthorpe Hall?"

"It matters naught. We shall spend very little time there. I detest the country." Estes's face was quite flushed now and his voice slightly slurred.

Tears welled up in Arabella's eyes. All of her illusions about marriage to Lord Estes were being slowly stripped away.

Seeing her tears, His Lordship observed coolly, "I am surprised to see that you are one of those women who cry when they are overjoyed. I hope you do not always do so, for I excessively dislike tears."

Arabella choked and, in a strangled voice, changed the subject: "Will all of your father's fortune go to you?"

"He would give anything to prevent it, but he can do nothing. I shall get his title and all of his great fortune. My inheritance was protected in the marriage settlement that my grandmother insisted upon when my parents married." Lord Estes grinned maliciously, his slate-blue eyes narrowing to mere slits. "God, how it must gall my dying father that I shall have his fortune—and the last laugh."

His Lordship snatched another glass of champagne from a footman, downed it in three gulps, and set the empty glass hard upon the table.

"My father would love to leave all he has to his bastard," Estes confided. "I suppose I do owe that ugly, stupid brute Damon thanks of a sort. He has eagerly slaved for our dear papa, making him far richer than he already was. Damon has greatly enlarged the fortune I shall inherit."

"If he has so increased your father's fortune, should he not receive something?"

"That mannerless peasant shall get nothing from me but my well-deserved contempt," His Lordship snapped.

Arabella wondered why His Lordship should hate his half brother so, when Estes would have everything and Damon nothing.

Standing up abruptly, Lord Estes said, "Let us go back to the assembly room."

Arabella readily agreed. She longed to escape his company now that she had discovered what a very different man he was from what she had thought.

In the hall, Estes suddenly opened a door to a small sitting room, pulled Arabella inside, and shut the door.

"What are you doing?" she demanded.

"We must have a kiss to seal our betrothal."

Reluctantly she closed her eyes. His hard, thin lips planted a dry kiss upon her mouth. She drew away in distaste. It was not at all like the passionate, devastating kiss that the midnight stranger had given her the previous night. Nor was her response. Estes evoked no dizzying sensations in her or longing to again feel his lips upon hers.

Chapter 7

Lord Estes Howard called upon Arabella's father the next morning, driving up in his curricle a scant ten minutes after Lord Vaughn returned home from Sussex. When Arabella was told that Estes was closeted with her father, her reaction was one of dread rather than delight. Her normally sparkling eyes were dulled by lack of sleep, and dark circles formed half-moons beneath them.

She had slept poorly, plagued by a dream in which the midnight stranger wrapped her in the comforting shelter of his arms and kissed her, a long, wonderful kiss that ended abruptly when Lord Estes stalked from a bog myrtle bush and shot the stranger dead. She had screamed and come awake to a frightened Beth shaking her.

Now as Arabella waited in her bedroom for her father and Lord Estes to finish their private meeting in the library, she felt no joy at her forthcoming marriage. All that she had discovered in the past thirty-six hours about herself and the man she was to marry had left her confused and anxious.

Lord Estes was no longer an enigma to her. She must marry him, of course. Having accepted Estes's offer, she could offer no satisfactory reason for suddenly reversing herself. But she would wed him out of duty and desperation, not desire.

He was her only hope for aiding Beth and Justin. And her family would be delighted by the match. Among the ton, a suitor's eligibility was determined by his title and fortune. His character, unless he was depraved, was almost incidental.

Arabella thought wistfully of the mysterious stranger and of his shattering kiss. She must stop dreaming of him. She could not jeopardize what everyone considered a brilliant match for a highly ineligible man whose name she did not even know, a man whom she most likely would never see again. Her heart seemed to snap at this thought.

When her father summoned her, Arabella obeyed with slow, reluctant steps. To her surprise, Lord Vaughn was alone in his library.

A pale shaft of light slanted through one of the clerestory windows, illuminating her father's weary face. Worried, unhappy lines seemed to be etching themselves more deeply into it with each passing day. His hair had thinned noticeably in recent weeks, and what was left of it had turned decidedly gray.

"Where is Lord Estes?" Arabella asked.

"He had an appointment with his tailor and had to leave," Lord Vaughn replied.

Arabella was irritated that her betrothed's tailor took precedence over her, yet relieved that she had not had to see Estes.

Her father said, "Of course the marriage is agreeable to you." It was a statement, not a question. "It is most agreeable to me as well. I hardly dared hope to see you married so well so cheaply. Lord Estes does not mind your lack of a dowry. You are very lucky, Arabella."

Until last night she would have agreed, but now she wondered.

"Why was Lord Estes here?" Lady Vaughn's querulous voice interjected. She had come into the library uninvited.

Her husband's face tightened, but he replied politely, "Lord Estes has made Arabella an offer."

"At last!" Despite her words, Lady Vaughn's face revealed that she was torn between delight at what this connection would do for her own consequence and jealousy that Arabella would become a very rich countess.

"It is a great honor, and one that the hoydenish chit has done nothing to deserve," Lady Vaughn proclaimed. "It is what I have worked so hard to obtain for her. I am, of course, a great favorite of Lord Estes's, and I flatter myself that I have played the crucial role in bringing this fine match off."

Arabella, remembering Lord Estes's dislike of her stepmother, longed to tell Lady Vaughn that she flattered herself far too much.

Her Ladyship continued. "You should be thankful, my lord, that you were so fortunate as to marry such a clever, managing woman as myself. I know of no other woman who would have done so much on behalf of a girl not even her own." Her Ladyship's tone turned peevish. "Of course, I shall have no thanks for my efforts from the ungrateful chit."

The ungrateful chit said nothing.

"I must begin planning the wedding at once," Lady Vaughn continued. "She will be married in London, of course. Everyone will be dangling after an invitation." She hurried from the room.

Arabella knew that she would be allowed no voice at all in her own wedding, but what disturbed her most was that her father could not afford the vulgar, outrageously expensive extravaganza that his wife would stage.

He must have had the same thought, for he flushed and cleared his throat. "Perhaps, Arabella, after you and Lord Estes are married, you can prevail upon him to help me out. I have so many pressing bills that must be settled."

Her face knitted in troubled surprise. "You want me to ask him to give you money?"

Lord Vaughn was spared having to reply by the arrival of Brom, still wearing a many-caped driving coat and gloves. Arabella's brother burst into the library like a whirlwind. He was a tall, gangling lad who had attained his growth in a sudden spurt that had left him far too thin. After his face and his body had a chance to fill out, he would be handsome, but now both were all skinny angles. His only outstanding feature was a pair of azure eyes the same shade as his sisters'.

"I must talk to you alone on a most urgent matter," Brom told his father. He turned to Arabella. "Would you leave us?"

She reluctantly acceded and shut the library door behind her. She had not even reached the stairs before she heard the voices of her father and brother raised in furious argument. She could not make out what they were saying through the thick oak door of the library, nor did she try. She continued up the stairs. As she was walking slowly down the hall toward her room, Brom suddenly dashed past her, nearly bowling her over, and ran into his room.

She followed him, shutting the door behind her. He had tossed his many-caped coat and gloves carelessly upon the bed and was staring stormily out the window.

"Brom, what is the matter?" she asked softly.

"I understand I should wish you happy," he said, turning sullen eyes toward her. They widened and softened when they saw her face. "Arabella, what is the matter? You don't look at all like a happy bride. Papa said you were pleased to be marrying Lord Estes; you don't look it. Frankly, I find him an awfully cold fish." Brom turned musingly back to the window. "I wonder if you will ever get to meet the earl's other son, the illegitimate one. They still talk about him and his wild escapades at Oxford and in the demimonde."

"What a great recommendation," Arabella said dryly. "What were you and Papa arguing about?"

Brom's face turned belligerent. "I must have five thousand pounds at once, and Papa refuses to give it to me."

Arabella was staggered. "But Brom, Papa does not have that kind of money."

Her brother's lower lip jutted out stubbornly. "He can raise it if he wants to."

Brom had been home so rarely in recent weeks that Arabella was not surprised he was unaware of his father's increasingly desperate financial situation. "No, Brom," she said gently. "Believe me, he cannot. He is so overextended that he is on the brink of ruin."

Brom's lower lip protruded even more prominently, making him look like a spoiled four-year-old, and he said bitterly, "If he is, it is because he has let that wretched wife of his squander his fortune."

Arabella went up to her brother, who was still standing by the window, and took his hands in hers. "What on earth can you need five thousand pounds for?"

"To save the dearest, sweetest little girl from a living hell." Brom's sullenness suddenly dissolved into the anguished concern that Arabella had seen when, as a younger boy, he had watched his dying mother suffer. "Oh, Arabella, it is the saddest, most dreadful story that you ever in your life heard."

And very likely the most untrue, Arabella thought. Even though she was certain that she knew the answer, she asked, "Who is the girl?"

"Her name is Julie Berner." Brom's face was flushed with the glow of a youth in the coils of first love. "She is the darlingest angel, Arabella."

His sister managed to conceal both her skepticism and her dismay. "What misfortune has befallen her?"

"Poor Julie's stepfather gambled away her mother's fortune and everything else the family had. He continued gambling even after he had nothing left. Finally he was forced to give Julie over to an evil old man named Amos Getz in payment of a debt of honor. Imagine, Arabella, her curst stepfather traded her honor for his own. Getz runs a, ah, gambling house in Covent Garden and wants to make poor Julie one of his women there.''

"How did you meet Julie?"

Brom blushed. "I, I happened into Getz's academy the night he got her. Poor little thing was cringing in a corner, and so unhappy. She told me she would kill herself if she were forced to remain there. I went to Getz, who said he would release her to me if I paid him the five thousand pounds her stepfather owed him. I told him that I would gladly do so but that I did not have that kind of blunt. He gave me until tonight to raise it. And I must, Arabella. I love her so. If only you could see the angel, you would adore her.''

Arabella was inclined to think that she would more likely strangle the calculating minx. Arabella was certain that her cousin Lance was right and that Brom was being gulled. Frowning, she asked, "How old is Julie?"

"Sixteen."

"So young! Are you certain?"

Brom's eyes glowed adoringly. "Oh, yes, she told me so."

Arabella stifled a groan. Her mama had once said that if she were asked to describe each of her children in one word, it would be impetuous for Arabella, sweet for Beth, and stubborn for Brom. Now he was so besotted over Julie that to tell him he was being hoaxed would only set his back up and make him even more intractable in his infatuation. So instead, Arabella, playing for time while she tried to think of what she could do to save him, said warmly, "How good and generous of you to want to rescue her, Brom."

"And I shall do so." His adolescent face radiated stubborn determination. "I must find someone to make me a loan.''

"Oh Brom," Arabella cried, thoroughly alarmed, "I beg of you, do not put yourself in the hands of moneylenders!"

"I must if I can raise the money no other way." He snatched up his many-caped coat from the bed. "And I have no time to lose." He vanished through the door, and she heard his footsteps running toward the stairs.

Arabella sank down upon his bed, remembering her promise to her mother to care for her two siblings. That promise was becoming increasingly difficult to keep. How could Arabella save Brom from his foolishness?

Arabella was as convinced as her cousin Lance that there was something very smoky about the affair. Julie must be in league with Amos Getz to relieve Brom of five thousand pounds. But why would they pick a penniless youth like her brother? There were plenty of rich sprigs in London who would make better picking than Brom.

Arabella desperately wished that she could talk to Mr. Smith. Surely he would know what she should do.

Chapter 8

Two hours after Lord Estes's curricle departed from the Vaughns', the duchess of Hampshire arrived in Arlington Street to see Arabella.

As Arabella entered the small withdrawing room where her aunt awaited her, the duchess said without preamble, "I hear that you have accepted Lord Estes's offer."

Arabella nodded, wondering if anything that transpired in London escaped her aunt's sharp ears.

"Why?"

"But Aunt Margaret," Arabella stammered as she shut the door behind her so that they could talk in private, "everyone thinks that Estes and I make a splendid match, uniting two such old and distinguished families."

"It is you and Lord Estes, not your families, who must live together. And what will you live on? You have no portion, and he is drowning in gambling debts."

"He is about to inherit his dying father's enormous fortune," Arabella reminded her.

"His father is no longer dying. The earl rallied three days ago, and his doctors say that he will live."

"How marvelous!" Arabella exclaimed, truly delighted that the earl was recovering.

"I wonder if Lord Estes thinks so," the duchess said, taking a seat on a small divan.

Probably not, Arabella thought, remembering with disgust the dreadful things her betrothed had said about his father.

The duchess gestured for her niece to sit beside her on the divan. "I so want, Arabella, to see you happily married to a man who loves and cherishes you."

Sitting down, Arabella asked in a small voice, "You don't think that Lord Estes loves me?"

"I think that Lord Estes loves himself too greatly to have much affection left over for anyone or anything else, except perhaps his clothes," her aunt said sarcastically. Her hand reached out and took one of her niece's in its strong grip. "Furthermore, you need a strong man. Do not make the mistake that your mama made!"

"What are you saying? Mama loved Papa!"

"Did she?" The duchess loosened her grip on Arabella's hand. "Your mama attracted suitors the way a hollyhock attracts bees, but none of them engaged her heart. Finally, when she was twenty-seven, our papa, fearing that she would end up on the shelf, told her that she must marry Lord Whittleson. She detested him, and rightly so. He was an evil man. To escape Whittleson, she married your papa." The duchess shook her head sadly. "But your mama was far too spirited for such a weak, dilatory man. She was not happy with him, although she never let him suspect it. She felt that she owed him at least that deception."

Her aunt's words gave Arabella insight for the first time into so much that had puzzled her about her parents' relationship. Her father's adoration of his wife had been transparent, but Arabella had sensed her mother's hidden unhappiness.

"You think that Lord Estes is weak," Arabella said, knowing in her heart that her aunt was right.

"He cannot help but be. He was raised by his mother, who spoiled him outrageously and refused even to let his father see him. I particularly dislike Henrietta. She is exactly like her mother, Lady Chatner, whose great fortune hooked her Lord Chatner. Not that he got any enjoyment of the money. The marriage settlement gave her control of it, and Chatner was the most henpecked man alive. He was so afraid of his wife that I think he would have preferred to walk through the fires of hell than to confront her."

Arabella reflected that their daughter Henrietta's marriage to the earl of Woodthorpe had been no happier. His wastrel father had been deeply in debt, and the ambitious Lady Chatner had seen an opportunity to make her daughter a countess. She would settle the father's debts if the son would marry Henrietta. But the son had fallen wildly in love with Nell Fitzhugh and would have none of it.

He eloped with Nell, but his father caught them and dragged the boy, who was still a month away from coming of age, home, where he was kept a prisoner for weeks until he finally agreed to marry Henrietta. Then he abandoned her to live with Nell.

Arabella could think of nothing more humiliating than to have one's own husband openly prefer another woman. "At least Lord Estes does not have his father's shocking morals," Arabella said tartly.

"But he is a gambler. Besides, Woodthorpe's morals were not shocking when he was young. When he lived with Nell Fitzhugh, no woman could have asked for a more devoted lover. He adored her and their son. It was only after her death that he turned to a string of lights-o'-love for comfort."

"You sound as though you rather admire Woodthorpe!" Arabella exclaimed in surprise.

"I do. I always admire strong men who succeed by their own endeavor. Woodthorpe's father had squandered the family's fortune. His son inherited only the title and Woodthorpe Hall. There was Henrietta's fortune, but under the marriage agreement, she retained control of it. To her astonishment, Woodthorpe refused to ask her for so much as a ha'penny.''

The duchess stared absently into space, the fingers of her right hand tapping lightly on the floral silk covering of the divan. "Then Woodthorpe was unexpectedly left Willow Wood, which at that time was a run-down little property. Somehow he managed to make it profitable. It was the base upon which he built his fortune without resorting to a shilling of Henrietta's.'' Her Grace sighed. "If only Estes had some of his father's strength and determination.''

Arabella said wistfully, "I wish that you had expressed your distaste for Lord Estes to me earlier.''

"It was not until I learned of Woodthorpe's feelings about Estes that I became thoroughly alarmed. I think highly of the earl's judgment. His antipathy toward Estes disturbs me more than anything else. I cannot like it, and I wish I knew what was behind it.''

"But Aunt Margaret, you said it is because of his gambling.''

"That is what my solicitor said. I do not believe it. I am certain that there is something more to it. Something quite dreadful. I wonder what it can be.''

The duchess mused in silence for a moment, then said, "Speaking of dreadful things, I hear that Lord Whittleson is buying up your father's debts.''

Arabella's azure eyes widened. "Why?''

"Revenge, no doubt. Whittleson has been nursing his hatred of your father ever since their duel.''

"But why has he done nothing until now?''

The duchess shrugged. "Could not afford it. He hadn't a feather to fly with for years, but recently he seems to have become very rich. There are nasty rumors that the sources of his income would not bear close scrutiny.''

Arabella twisted her hands anxiously. "What do you think Whittleson means to do to Papa?"

"Put him in debtors' prison."

The color drained from Arabella's face. If that happened, her father would be desperate enough to give in to Lady Vaughn's scheme to marry Beth to Rufus Dobbs.

An hour after the duchess of Hampshire's departure, a side door of Lord Vaughn's house opened. The slim figure of a woman in a green redingote trimmed with bands of velvet and a large, wide-brimmed bonnet slipped outside. Her face was concealed beneath the heavy veil she wore. She hurried up the path that ran along the house to the street and around the corner, where she sighed in audible relief at the sight of the hackney that often waited there.

Going up to its driver, a middle-aged man with a kindly face, she said, "I wish to hire you."

The man looked at her sharply. Young ladies of quality did not hire hackneys and drive off without abigails, even when their faces were concealed behind heavy veils. But a fare was a fare, and he nodded.

After she was settled in his vehicle, he sustained a far more severe shock when she announced that her destination was Mr. Amos Getz's establishment in Covent Garden.

"Me cannot take ye there," he protested.

"Don't you know the address?" the lady inquired in a voice muffled by her veil.

He knew the address very well, for he had delivered to Getz's "academy" from time to time drunken, rackety bucks, but never before had he been asked to take a female, least of all a young lady of obvious quality, to such a disreputable place.

"You cannot want to go there," he persisted. "It is no place for a lady. Me cannot take you."

"But you must," the muffled voice cried in acute distress. "I go on an errand of great urgency. I will pay you well."

When the driver showed no sign of yielding, she cried recklessly, "I will pay double your usual fare."

Greed warred with conscience in the coachman. Greed won. Conscience, however, attached a caveat to his agreement: "But only if you permit me to wait for you there and bring you back here."

"How nice of you to offer," she cried. "I should like that very much indeed."

The decidedly young timbre of her voice added to the coachman's misgivings, but he climbed up on his box and started off.

Inside Arabella thought of her coming confrontation with Julia Coates, alias Julie Berner. Arabella planned to disclose that she was wise to the scheme to bilk Brom out of five thousand pounds and to threaten Miss Coates with legal retribution if she pursued it.

By the time the hackney stopped in front of Mr. Getz's academy, the coachman's misgivings had grown to sufficient proportions that instead of opening the door to let Arabella alight, he held it firmly shut. He requested that he be permitted to handle her errand while she waited in the hackney.

Neither he nor his passenger noticed the impressive figure of a man in a dashing blue carrick emerge from the building next to Getz's and saunter down the steps.

Arabella rejected the coachman's offer. "I must do it myself. Be so kind as to open the door."

At the sound of her voice, the man on the steps stopped abruptly, and his deep brown eyes stared in horrified surprise at the hackney.

"Ma'am, me wish you would not go in there," the driver pleaded.

"Sir," she said firmly, "open the door this instant."

The coachman reluctantly obeyed. Arabella's regal figure

emerged. She started for Mr. Getz's steps, only to find her way blocked by a pair of extraordinarily broad shoulders encased in a blue carrick cut in the very latest style.

Startled, Arabella tilted her head upward to view the face above the shoulders and found herself staring into the dark eyes of the stranger whose kiss had enthralled her. Her heart thumped wildly and a tiny, involuntary gurgle of delight escaped her lips. "Oh, I so wanted to see you," she breathed.

He, however, did not look at all as if he wanted to see her. In fact, he looked furious.

"What the devil do you think you are doing here?" he demanded roughly, his brown eyes snapping with anger. "What about your solemn oath to me that you would do nothing outrageous like this again?"

Arabella was dumbfounded by his anger. "But I am not doing anything—" she stammered.

"You see nothing outrageous about marching up the front steps of the most infamous brothel and gambling hell in London, and in broad daylight at that! You ninnyhammer, no decent woman in her right mind would enter that door! Nothing could sink your reputation faster."

Her face flamed beneath her veil, and her stricken gaze fell away from his enraged eyes.

"Me tried to tell her," the hackney driver interjected helpfully, "but she would not listen."

"Undoubtedly she would not!" the stranger snapped. "Get back into the hackney instantly before someone happens by and recognizes you."

"No one will know me with this veil," Arabella protested.

"I did," he pointed out curtly, "and so may others. Get in!"

Dumbly she obeyed him. He got in after her and told the driver, "Take us back to Arlington Street at once."

"No, I must see Julia Coates," Arabella protested. "She is gulling Brom."

"You won't find Julia Coates at Amos Getz's. She's a much more expensive bit of fluff than that."

"She told Brom that she was being kept there against her will."

"Your brother is even more crackbrained than you if he believed that bouncer. Now tell me why you came here today."

Arabella did. By the time she finished, her companion's anger had cooled. He said quietly, "I will take care of Brom and Miss Coates for you."

Arabella wanted to cry with relief. Still, she protested, "But you have done so much for me already. I do not wish to embroil you—"

"But I wish to be embroiled." He gave her such an irresistible smile that her heart began to race.

"Brom is very difficult to handle," she warned.

Mr. Smith grinned at her. "Undoubtedly, since he is your brother."

"Julie has convinced Brom that she is an innocent angel," Arabella said. "He will not believe you if you try to tell him the truth about Julie."

"I do not plan to try to tell him."

"But what will you do? If you do not convince him of her perfidy, he will continue to worship her."

"Trust me." His brown eyes, as soft as velvet, smiled reassuringly at her. "Where can I find Brom?"

Arabella gave him the address of Elton Davies's rooms where her brother often stayed, then complained, "Since Brom never comes home anymore, I suppose I shall not know for days whether you are successful."

He smiled. "I shall deliver him to you tonight in Arlington Street with his eyes opened to his angel's perfidy."

"That is impossible!" she protested, a suspicion growing in her that now she was the one being hoaxed.

"Trust me. Did I fail you before?"

"No," she admitted. Suddenly a disconcerting question struck her. "What were *you* doing at such a notorious spot as Mr. Getz's?" she demanded.

"I was not at Getz's. I was next door on an errand for my father." He raised a triangular eyebrow. "And do not ask me what the errand was. That is confidential."

A mischievous grin suddenly played at the corners of his mouth. "I do have a question of you, however. Do you have any other siblings who might require assistance in their affairs of the heart? If so, I think it is only fair that you warn me now."

For the first time that day, Arabella laughed.

"That's better," he said approvingly. "I was beginning to think I should never see your delightful dimples again."

The dimples were much in evidence as she thought how happy she was when she was with him. She relaxed against the cushion, confident that he would take care of Brom for her.

As they bounced along in the poorly sprung hackney, she was achingly conscious of her companion's nearness to her on the narrow seat. How much finer a figure he was than Lord Estes. Depression engulfed her at the thought of her betrothal. Her aunt was right. She needed a strong man that she could love and respect. *And that man sat beside her.*

Twilight was descending upon the vehicle, casting her companion's face in shadows. She longed to see him more clearly and started to raise her veil so that she might do so.

"No!" He seized her hands and pulled them away from the veil. "Leave it alone. We dare not chance that you be recognized with me. It would be as bad for your reputation as being seen entering Amos Getz's." His voice was light, but his eyes were very serious.

He signaled the coachman to stop. The wheels had not yet stopped rolling when he opened the door, jumped gracefully down, and closed the door again. "Go on," he ordered the coachman. "Do not stop until you have delivered her in Arlington Street."

The coach rolled forward before Arabella could protest, and he vanished into the twilight.

Chapter 9

⤞

Bromley Vaughn arrived at Elton Davies's rooms that evening with shoulders slumped in dejection.

From all the tales that Brom had heard about greedy moneylenders, he had assumed that they would be only too eager to lend him any sum that he desired so long as the interest was sufficiently usurious. But during the last few hours he had learned that their eagerness did not extend to an eighteen-year-old without any property to his name and a father who was well known to be very badly sprung himself. Brom had not been able to raise a guinea, and tonight was Amos Getz's deadline.

Brom dreaded the thought of having to face his beloved Julie and confess that he had failed. His only hope was to convince Getz to extend his deadline.

Brom was thankful that Elton had gone to Bath for two weeks to attend his mother, who was taking the waters there. Brom had no desire to have to converse with anyone. So it came as an unhappy surprise to him to discover a stranger sitting in Elton's parlor.

"Who the devil are you, and what are you doing here?" Brom demanded.

"The landlady let me in," the stranger said, laying aside

his book and rising to his feet. "I presume you are Bromley Vaughn."

Brom nodded, staring up in astonishment at his visitor. The man was a giant both in height and physique, and damned handsome, too. He was elegantly dressed in the first stare of fashion but without any hint of peacockishness. Brom was certain that no one but Weston himself could have tailored that superb frock coat of blue superfine.

"I am here," the tall stranger said, "because of Miss Julie Berner. I am hoping we can join forces to effect her immediate removal from Amos Getz's establishment."

Brom felt a wild surge of jealousy, then a strong dislike of the handsome stranger, and he blustered, "What is Julie to you?"

"Nothing, nothing at all," the stranger assured him blandly. "That is why I am here."

"I don't understand. If she is nothing—"

The stranger raised a silencing hand. "I am disgusted that a young girl might be forced into such a life against her will. I have a plan for freeing her, but if I implement it, I shall have her on my hands, and I do not want that."

"Why not?" Brom demanded suspiciously. He was convinced that no sane man could resist his beloved Julie, and his visitor did not look at all addled.

The man cocked a triangular black eyebrow and asked incredulously, "A girl of sixteen? I am thirty-two, twice her age. I am no cradle robber."

Brom was mollified. "Yes, of course, you are *quite elderly*."

"Quite," the stranger agreed, a hint of laughter deep in his dark eyes. "But I understand that you, sir, have very honorable intentions toward Miss Berner. I was thinking that once I secured her freedom, you could relieve me of the responsibility for her."

"Oh yes!" Brom cried joyously, deciding that he liked his

caller after all. But his euphoria gave way almost at once to suspicion. "But why would you pay five thousand pounds to save a girl that you have no interest in?"

His visitor grinned. "I do not propose that either of us pay Amos Getz so much as a shilling."

"Not a shilling!" Brom was dazed by the man's audacity. "I do not even know your name, Mr.—Mr.?"

"Smith, Howard Smith. But do not call me Mr. Smith tonight at Getz's. For my plan to work, we must appear to be the closest of friends. Now here is what we shall do."

Bromley Vaughn's arrival at Amos Getz's establishment was noted with a triumphant smile by a stocky man watching the street from an upper window. The man, whose hair was more gray than black, had a harsh, heavily lined face set with narrow, calculating eyes. A whitened scar ran diagonally from near his ear to the corner of his mouth, giving him a sinister appearance despite the richness of his evening clothes.

He turned from the window to the room's other occupant, a petite young girl who looked as though she were still in the schoolroom. The beauty and innocence of her heart-shaped face made one instantly think of angels. Great violet eyes looked up meltingly from beneath her lashes. Blond hair had been arranged in a halo about her head that enhanced the angelic illusion. She wore a white muslin gown that also had been cleverly designed to accentuate her innocent appearance.

They were in a small paneled office dominated by a large carved mahogany desk, its top strewn messily with papers. Stepping away from the window, the man announced, "Your pigeon is here, Julia."

The girl pouted, erasing from her face in a single stroke the illusion of both extreme youth and innocence. "Young

Vaughn is such a bore. I do not understand why you wish me
to play this charade with a calfling.''

The man's eyes narrowed to mere slits, and his voice was
frigid. ''I have told you before, Julia, yours is not to understand but to do as I wish. Remember, if you succeed, you will
be richly rewarded.''

He went to the big desk, pulled out a drawer, and removed
a long velvet box. Opening it, he revealed a dazzling necklace set with dozens of small, perfectly cut diamonds. From
this circle of precious stones hung, pendant-fashion, a huge,
many-carat diamond of flawless perfection.

Julia stared at the necklace with greedy eyes.

The man watched her with amusement. He lifted the necklace from its box and held it up before her face so that the
multitude of diamonds sparkled in the lamplight. ''You are
a fine actress, my dear Julia. Look upon tonight as one of the
most important performances of your life. If you succeed, you
will have two of your greatest desires: you will own this
necklace, and you will be rid of young Vaughn.''

''He will not have the five thousand pounds tonight,'' she
protested impatiently.

''Of course he will not. But it is your task to make him so
desperate over the dreadful plight of his darling, adoring angel that he will jump at the opportunity of my loaning it to
him. I am counting upon you, Julia.'' The harsh face hardened into cruel lines. ''Do not disappoint me. I am not nice
to people who do so.''

His threat was not wasted on Julia. ''I won't disappoint
you,'' she promised uneasily. ''But if you loan him the
money and he gives it to Amos, he will think that I belong to
him.''

''Of course he will. Furthermore, once his note to me is
duly signed and witnessed, you and he will go off together in
a coach of my providing.''

''I will do no such thing! That penniless fool wants to

marry me!'' Julia grimaced at such a wretchedly distasteful possibility.

The man ignored her protest and continued smoothly. ''Before you leave, you will get him to drink a toast to you and to his success in rescuing you. Do not join him. By the time the coach has gone a mile, he will be unconscious. When he awakes, he will find himself beaten and robbed in one of our lovely city's most squalid slums. And Miss Julie Berner will have vanished forever.'' His lips twisted into an ugly smile. ''But young Vaughn's debt to me will remain.''

Brom was admitted to Getz's by a great brute of a man. His ugly face was dominated by a flattened nose, the lower portion of which turned peculiarly to the right.

''Good evening, Groot,'' Brom said uneasily. Groot's disposition was as ugly as his face. On the first night that Brom had come here, he had witnessed Groot beating a patron who had run afoul of him. It had been a sickening sight, and Brom had been careful since then to be very polite to Groot.

The hall in which Groot presided was lined with doors, each of which led to a different pleasure, depending upon one's tastes. Brom went to a gambling saloon near the front of the building. He opened the door and stepped inside. Various games of chance were in progress about the room. One end was dominated by a faro table. Brom recognized none of the gamblers. Neither Julie nor Getz was in sight.

Tables had been scattered about the room for the convenience of gamesters. Two waiters hovered unobtrusively in the background, seeing that players were well supplied with wine that would blunt their caution.

Brom wandered over by the faro table. There was no sign of Mr. Smith, who was to meet Brom here. A disquieting thought struck Brom. Groot was very careful about whom he let in. What if he barred Mr. Smith?

Julie floated into the room, looking more angelic than Brom had ever seen her, and came up to him.

"Oh, Brom, Brom, my darling," she cried in a low, wispy voice, her face radiant, "I was so terrified that you would not come tonight."

She was less than five feet tall. Brom, who had passed the six-foot mark, towered above her. She smiled sadly up at him, whispering, "Every moment today seemed to pass as slowly as an eternity for me. Mr. Getz insisted that you would not come for me tonight, that you would abandon me rather than pay him the money. Oh, Brom!" Tears welled up in her violet eyes. She tilted her head down and looked up at Brom beseechingly through her lashes and tears.

Her unhappiness made Brom so wretched that he felt as if his own heart were breaking.

She continued in a voice trembling with emotion. "You cannot know what agonies I have suffered today wondering if you would come."

"Surely you knew I would," Brom protested.

"Oh, I wanted so to believe it, but Mr. Getz . . ." She took Brom's hands into her own tiny ones and confessed in a tremulous voice, "I had decided that if you did not come tonight with the money that I would kill myself!"

Her little chin tilted dramatically upward, and through lashes glistening with tears, she looked at him with tragic determination. "I would rather be dead than live—" She broke off as a violent shudder convulsed her delicate frame.

Brom was so distressed by his love's suffering that he could scarcely keep the tears from his own eyes.

"Oh," she shuddered suddenly, gesturing toward the rear of the room, where a dark little man with an oily smile had appeared in a small doorway. "It is Mr. Getz."

Brom took her hands in his. "My darling, you need worry yourself about him no longer."

"You have the money?" Her ethereal voice was a mere wisp.

He nodded.

Teary eyelids flew open, revealing startled violet eyes. "You do?" she demanded in a tone that seemed more horrified than pleased.

Brom had no time to reflect upon this, however, for Mr. Getz was coming toward them. And at that very moment, Mr. Smith appeared in the door that led from the entrance hall. His arrival caused an unusual stir among the gamblers. Normally they paid no attention to new arrivals, but several tables paused in their play to stare at him as he sauntered languidly toward Brom. The observers whispered among themselves, their eyes still fastened on the newcomer's imposing figure. No one in the room was staring more fixedly than Amos Getz, who had stopped dead at the sight of him.

Mr. Smith bowed to Julie, who also seemed to be transfixed. "Ah, Miss—"

"Berner," she interjected hastily, giving the newcomer a pregnant look. "Julie Berner."

Howard lifted a triangular eyebrow questioningly at her, then said, "I see that you know my dear friend Bromley Vaughn."

Her pale skin grew even paler. She opened her mouth but was saved from having to say anything by the arrival at her side of Amos Getz.

Seeing him, Mr. Smith said affably, "Amos Getz, so we meet again after so long a time. What a pleasure."

Getz looked as though it were anything but a pleasure. Frowning, he demanded, "Did Groot let you in?" Getz's tone implied his henchman would regret this mistake.

"But of course," Mr. Smith said with a lazy smile. "He has grown in wisdom as well as age since last I saw him." The smile broadened. "You no doubt have observed the abrupt right turn his nose makes in the course of its journey down his face.''

''What has that to do with anything?'' snapped Getz.

''It was my pleasure to arrange that for him some years ago after he and I had a difference of opinion over my entry into the establishment where he then worked.''

''Why are you here?'' Getz demanded hostilely.

His tone startled Brom. Normally Getz's voice dripped oily welcome to all who came within his doors and especially to a man so obviously flush in the pockets as Mr. Smith.

Mr. Smith smiled. ''I had a strong yearning for a few hands of piquet with someone shrewd enough to make the game interesting. I immediately thought of you. You will, of course, accommodate me.'' This final sentence was delivered more in the nature of an order than a request.

Getz nodded reluctantly.

Mr. Smith turned to Brom. ''Will you and Miss Berner do me the honor of accompanying me?''

''Of course,'' Brom said uneasily. He wished that Mr. Smith had told him that piquet was his game. Brom would have warned him that he had yet to see anyone win at it against Mr. Getz.

''Brom, what about the money?'' Julie asked desperately.

Before he could answer, Mr. Smith interposed, ''Miss, ah, ah—what did you say it was, Berner?—you will be so kind as to join Brom and me. I am convinced the presence of such an *angelic lady*''—the peculiar inflection he gave to these two words caused Julie to turn slightly green—''must bring me luck.''

Julie looked frantically about as though to escape. But Mr. Smith took her arm firmly, so firmly that she winced, and led her to one of the small tables.

Chapter 10

Brom, his thin face drawn in a troubled frown, followed Julie and Mr. Smith to the table. He was not such a flat that he did not recognize that something was going on of which he was ignorant. But he could not plumb the depths of the tense undercurrents that swirled about him.

Getz sat down across the table from Mr. Smith. Ignoring the two packs of cards that already lay at one corner of the table, Getz pulled two other packs from the pocket of his frock coat, broke one open, and laid it on the table.

"If you please." Mr. Smith took the cards, studied them closely as he riffled through the deck, then returned them to Getz.

"I trust," Mr. Smith said in a tone of cold steel that was at odds with his affable smile, "that you will not try any of your old tricks tonight. You will remember what I promised you the last time you were so foolish as to try them on me."

Getz's eyes bulged as though he were standing in a hangman's noose.

"Now that we understand each other, let us get on with the play," Mr. Smith said coolly.

"What stakes do you want?" Getz asked.

"At least enough to make it interesting," Mr. Smith said

carelessly. "Say five hundred pounds a game and another five hundred for a capot."

Julie gasped; Getz winced but agreed to the stakes.

Brom's confusion gave way to dismay. Mr. Smith was clearly mad. Never had Brom seen such high stakes at piquet, and especially not against Amos Getz, who never lost at it. Mr. Smith would never be able to pull off his plan.

But once again Brom was surprised. Mr. Smith's play could be described only as brilliant—and ruthless. True, Lady Luck seemed to be running with him, but he made the most of the lady's benevolence. Several of the games were decided in a single hand. Mr. Smith thrice scored a capot, and Getz was lurched a half-dozen times.

Several times Julie tried to break away from Mr. Smith's side. But each time, his restraining hand snaked out to stop her, and he would say, "You really must stay, Miss Berner. You bring me such good luck."

When Mr. Smith called a halt to the play, his winnings stood at eight thousand pounds.

When Getz, looking white and shaken, paid off in a thick stack of bank notes, Mr. Smith separated five thousand pounds from them and handed the money to Brom. "Here is the loan that I promised you, Brom. Give it to Mr. Getz to free your love from his odious clutches."

Ecstatic, Brom turned to Julie and cried, "My darling angel, you are saved."

He tried to embrace her, but to his astonishment, she shoved him away with more strength than he would ever have dreamed her tiny form possessed. "What is it?" Brom stammered.

She ignored him and asked Mr. Smith in a voice far harder than Brom had ever heard from her lips before, "Why are you giving him the money?"

Mr. Smith smiled broadly. "It's my wedding present to you. He told me that it was your dearest wish to marry him."

Julie looked as though her dearest wish were to murder Mr. Smith.

"We, we must toast this happy event," Amos Getz said hastily. He ignored a waiter who was passing nearby with several glasses of champagne and beckoned instead to one who stood against the wall as though awaiting his summons.

Brom noticed Mr. Smith's eyes narrow as the second waiter hurried up with two glasses of claret upon the tray.

"Will you have one?" Brom said to Julie.

"No, no," she said hastily. "I never drink wine."

"You don't!" Mr. Smith exclaimed in a tone that implied he knew otherwise. Suddenly he turned, reached out, and snatched two glasses of champagne from the other waiter's tray. He handed one to Brom, who was reaching for a glass of claret. "Take the champagne, Brom," Mr. Smith said firmly. "We will drink no paltry claret to toast such a momentous occasion as this. Only champagne will do." He held up a glass to Julie and Brom.

"I prefer claret," Julie snapped.

Mr. Smith's eyes glittered dangerously. "Then drink it." With his free hand, he took one of the clarets and offered it to her.

She backed away as though he were giving her a hemlock cup. "No, no, I want nothing!"

Mr. Smith offered the claret to Amos Getz, but he also declined it. A grim hint of a smile played at the corners of Mr. Smith's mouth as he returned the unwanted claret to the waiter's tray.

Brom raised his champagne glass. With a glowing smile at Julie, he said, "To my bride!" He had planned to give voice to further loving encomiums to his bride's heavenly beauty and sweetness, but he was startled into silence by the anger that erased her angelic countenance. It was as if Brom were seeing the face of a stranger, a much older, harder woman whom he did not recognize. The tiniest of doubts about his bride-to-be flickered deep in his breast. Hastily he gulped down his champagne as if to douse that insidious little flame.

Mr. Smith said, "Come, Brom and Miss Co—ah, Berner—my carriage is awaiting us outside."

Julie backed away. "No, no, I cannot go off alone with two men. My reputation would be ruined."

This seemed too much for Mr. Smith's composure, and he burst out laughing. Julie glared at him.

Still grinning, he assured her that she had nothing to fear. "I have here in my coat a special license for you to wed Brom, and a minister waiting even now to perform the ceremony this very night. We go to him directly." He added, as though an afterthought to himself, "Of course, Brom does not have a feather to fly with, but what is money when you have love?"

"Indeed, Julie, how happy we—" Brom began, but he was struck speechless in midsentence by the transformation before his eyes of his beloved angel into a furious hellcat. Gone was her wispy little voice, and in its place was a shrill screech that would have done a fishmonger proud.

"You bastard!" she screamed at Mr. Smith.

"Julie," Brom cried in shock, trying to take her arm.

She slapped it away, wheeled on him, and shrieked insults that disparaged his birth, his character, and his manhood in language not usually heard this side of Billingsgate.

Brom stared at her with the stricken eyes of a man who has seen the woman he worshiped not merely slip from the pedestal upon which he had placed her but plunge headlong into the gutter. His voice failed him, and he thought for a moment that his breaking heart would do the same.

Mr. Smith stepped forward, grabbed Julie by the arms, and shook her, saying, "That will do, Miss Coates."

She broke away from him and fled.

Mr. Smith took Brom's arm and said gently, "Let us go."

The dazed Brom allowed himself to be led outside and into his companion's carriage.

As it rumbled off, Brom asked brokenly, "You called her Miss Coates. Is she really Julia Coates?"

"Yes, I am afraid she is."

Brom was overwhelmed by her perfidy. What a fool he had been. Not only was the innocent girl that he had adored neither innocent nor a girl, but she had deliberately played him false. In a voice edged with grief and disillusionment, he said, "My cousin Lance told me that was her real name and that she was a notorious demirep, but I didn't believe him." He turned savagely on Mr. Smith. "You knew, didn't you."

"Who she was? Yes. I first met her when she was under Lord Black's protection nearly a decade ago."

"So long ago!" Brom exclaimed, the agony in his heart beginning to give way to anger at the heartless, lying woman who had made such a fool of him. "But she told me that she was sixteen."

"Only one of many lies that she told you," his companion gently pointed out.

Brom was so angry and humiliated that he lashed out at Mr. Smith. "Why didn't you tell me that she was gulling me!"

"Because you would not have believed me," Mr. Smith said quietly. His look of understanding and sympathy cooled Brom's anger toward him.

"No, I guess I would not have," Brom acknowledged bitterly. He deserved to be the laughingstock of London.

"Had I been in your place," Mr. Smith continued, "I undoubtedly would not have believed me either, so why should I expect more of you?"

Brom's charred self-esteem began to rise from its ashes at this statement. He admitted in a broken voice, "I was so wild about her. I thought she was an angel from heaven."

Grimacing at his own stupidity, he thought of the tirade

that his father had delivered to him earlier that day. Brom's belated recognition of the wisdom of those comments only increased his humiliation. He said bitterly, "What a cake she made of me. No doubt you will tell me what a good lesson this is for me."

"I will tell you nothing so silly as that!" Mr. Smith assured him. "Heartbreak is never a good lesson. It is a very bad one. Unfortunately it is one none of us escapes."

"I wish you were my father," Brom cried, grateful for his companion's compassion. "What sermons Papa will read me about the stupid follies of youth."

"Youth has no monopoly on foolish follies of the heart. A great many men far more advanced in years and experience than you have been fooled by a deceiving petticoat, even your father. At least you have not been permanently entrapped, as he is with your stepmother."

Brom stared in surprise at the stranger. It was the first time that he had met a man some years older than himself who talked to him as though they were equals instead of with condescending superiority. Suddenly what Mr. Smith thought of him assumed utmost, if illogical, importance in Brom's mind. He said bitterly, "You must think me a cawker."

"Not at all! You must not be so hard on yourself, Brom. You were clearly the object of a very carefully laid plot."

"By whom?"

"The owner of that establishment. Julia Coates has been living under his protection for some months now, and he used her to bait the trap."

"I cannot believe that she is Getz's mistress!"

"She isn't. Getz does not own the academy."

"Who does?"

"Lord Whittleson."

"Papa's enemy?"

"Precisely. I suspect he would have appeared tonight to offer you a loan of the five thousand pounds. Once he had your note, he would have added it to the other debts of your father's that he is buying up in an attempt to put your papa into debtors' prison.''

"My God," Brom cried, truly shocked. "If it had not been for you . . .'' He broke off and frowned at his benefactor. Brom had experienced humiliating disillusionment tonight, and now he was suspicious of everyone. "Why did you come to me? Why did you go to so much trouble for a stranger?''

"It has been a very profitable evening for me. I am three thousand pounds richer.''

"You would have been eight thousand richer if you had gone there on your own," Brom pointed out.

His companion smiled. "But I would not have done so. I do not gamble.''

"You are roasting me! I've never seen anyone play as you did tonight. You cannot tell me that you have never gambled.''

"I did not tell you that. In my wild, younger days, I did a great many things that no longer hold any interest for me.'' Laughter trembled in his voice. "After all, as you pointed out earlier this evening, I am quite elderly.''

Brom blushed, but he was not to be diverted. "Why did you come to me this evening?''

"A friend told me your story, and I was intrigued by it. You remind me a bit of myself. I was about your age when my mother, whom I adored, died. I took her loss very hard, and I rebelled.'' Mr. Smith's brown eyes were brooding and he gave a mirthless laugh. "I could not begin to list all of the crazy, foolish things that I did.''

It was a unique experience for Brom to have a man older than himself display such understanding and to confess his own failings besides. What a prime gun Mr. Smith was! But who could have told him about Brom? The youth voiced his question aloud.

"I am sorry, but I cannot reveal that. I am sworn to protect the confidence. I can tell you only that it was someone who recognized what was being done to you and longed to help you see the truth.''

Brom leaned his head back on the carriage's soft cushions. ''How can I ever repay you?''

''By doing three very simple things,'' his companion replied promptly. ''First, promise me that you will never go near Amos Getz's again. It is for your own safety. Whittleson is a mean loser. So is Getz.''

Brom readily agreed. Having seen the damage Groot could do to a man, Brom was not eager to test what his reception would be at Getz's.

''Second,'' Mr. Smith continued, ''go home tonight to Arlington Street, and third, don't ask me why I request you to do so.''

''But—'' Brom started to protest.

Mr. Smith raised his hand to silence Brom. ''That is all that I ask of you,'' he said firmly. ''It is not a great deal. Will you indulge me?''

Brom nodded reluctantly.

A minute later the carriage stopped in front of the Vaughn house. Mr. Smith said, ''I must ask you to step out quickly. Thanks to our adventures tonight, I am quite late for an engagement with a lady who is not known for her patience.'' Mr. Smith gave Brom a warm, coaxing smile. ''I beg of you not to make me any later than I already am.''

Brom hastily obeyed, and the carriage vanished around the corner.

Arabella was alone in the library, trying in vain to concentrate on the page in front of her. Had she been asked what it said, she would have been unable to answer or even to give the title of the book in her hands. Her mind was completely absorbed by whether Mr. Smith would be able to keep his promise to bring Brom home tonight.

To her surprise, she heard the front door open. It was far too early to be Brom, but she went to the door of the library anyway. To her amazement, it was her brother.

"Brom," she called softly to him.

He came to her, a smile on his face. Arabella's heart sank. The midnight stranger had failed her. Brom was too happy to have had his Julia's perfidy exposed to him.

Brom led her back into the library. "I was hoping you would still be up to talk to," he told her in a voice brimming with excitement. "I have met the most prime gun today."

"Prime gun" was Brom's highest accolade. Arabella stared at him in astonishment. "But what happened with Julie?"

His eyes glinted angrily, but his words were careless. "She was not what I thought. She was hoaxing me."

"Oh, Brom, I am sorry." Arabella wrapped her arm around her brother to comfort him. "Is your heart broken?"

"It was at first," Brom admitted. "But after talking to Mr. Smith, I feel much better."

"Mr. Smith?" she asked faintly, releasing her brother.

"He is the prime gun I was talking about!"

Arabella's heart leaped with excitement. He had not failed her after all!

She led Brom to a sofa and seated herself beside him, saying, "Tell me everything that has happened since I saw you this afternoon."

Brom complied and concluded by telling her Mr. Smith's destination after Arlington Street. Arabella instantly conceived an antipathy, as enormous as it was inexplicable, for a certain impatient lady.

Brom said, "I wish Mr. Smith could disclose who told him about me, but he is too honorable a man to break his word."

Arabella gave silent thanks that Mr. Smith had not revealed her secret. She tried to keep her voice calm as she asked, "Who is this Mr. Smith? Where does he live?"

Brom stared at her with a startled expression. "You know, I never found out! We were so busy talking about me that I learned very little about him, not even where he lives."

Arabella bit her lips in frustration. Would the midnight stranger's identity remain forever a mystery to her?

Chapter 11

"No one can remember anything like it before," the duchess of Hampshire said to Arabella. "London can talk of nothing else."

The two were sitting together on the floral divan in the small withdrawing room of the Vaughn residence. They, like the rest of London, were discussing the earl of Woodthorpe's shocking announcement after his escape from death's door.

"Have you talked to Estes about it?" the duchess asked.

"No, I have not seen him since the night two weeks ago that he made his offer," Arabella confessed, embarrassed by his inattention.

"How very odd," her aunt said, echoing Arabella's own sentiment. "After all, you are his betrothed."

"I cannot believe that I shall be for much longer. He can no longer afford to marry a girl without a portion."

"I am certain you are right. How hard this must be for you."

Arabella looked down guiltily at her hands resting on the lap of her yellow Jacquard silk gown and said nothing. She could not bring herself to confess even to her aunt that the thought of being rid of Estes delighted rather than pained her.

"Such a scandal!" the duchess exclaimed. "Woodthorpe

could not have reaped more attention if he had taken an advertisement in the *Gazette*."

The earl's stunning statement, issued through his solicitor, bared a long-hidden scandal surrounding Woodthorpe's marriage to the countess Henrietta. It also disclosed that Lord Estes Howard was much misinformed about the size of the fortune he would inherit upon the earl's death. Only Woodthorpe Hall and the small estate attached to it, a tiny fraction of Woodthorpe's vast holdings, were entailed. And that was all Estes would receive.

To insure this, the earl had already signed over the rest of his estates and fortune to Damon Howard, his son by Nell Fitzhugh.

Nor was Damon, according to the statement, illegitimate. He had been conceived after a lawful marriage between his parents at Gretna Green. Contrary to the story given out by the earl's father at the time, he had not reached the eloping couple until two weeks after they had been married.

The desperate father had managed in great haste and secrecy to have the union annulled on the grounds it had never been consummated. But Damon's birth nine months and four days after the wedding refuted this claim. It also threw into confusion the legality of an annulment that had been obtained by false statements and on fraudulent grounds.

In short, there was a question as to which of the earl's sons was legitimate, although there was none at all as to which was now poor.

"Woodthorpe has had the last laugh on his countess," the duchess said. "How very clever he was."

"But Estes said the marriage settlement assured that everything would go to him," Arabella said.

"As Old Lady Chatner had it written, it did," replied the duchess, who had lost no time in extracting the full story from her solicitor, who was also the earl's. "But Woodthorpe adamantly refused to marry Henrietta unless the provision was changed to include only the estate he would inherit from his father and whatever additions to it resulted from Henrietta's fortune.''

"Was Henrietta not informed of the change?'' Arabella asked.

"No, nor was her mother. The two women were making poor Chatner's existence so miserable for not securing the marriage that he agreed to the change without saying a word to either of them. Since Woodthorpe was penniless, Chatner thought it would not matter, because everything of necessity must come from Henrietta's money.''

"But he was wrong,'' Arabella observed, raising her voice to be heard above a sudden babble of children's voices that rose up from the street. The day was exceptionally warm, and the windows of the withdrawing room, which faced the street, had been thrown open. Now the noise of the street as well as air drifted through them.

The duchess said, "Chatner had not reckoned on his son-in-law's later inheritance of Willow Wood or Woodthorpe's genius for making money. Now it is clear why the earl was so excessively careful all those years never to touch a penny of Henrietta's money.''

"But why did Woodthorpe never reveal any of this before?'' Arabella asked her aunt. "It was unfair to Lord Estes to let him think he would inherit a great fortune.''

"But he would have. My solicitor says the earl had always planned to divide his estate equally between his two sons, even though Damon was his favorite. But something happened just before the earl took ill that so turned him against Estes that he gave Damon everything he could. And by raising the question of the annulment's legality, the earl has even cast a shadow over Estes's claim to the title.''

Arabella heard the sound of a carriage stopping in front of the house. Surely it could not be Lady Vaughn returning already from a shopping expedition with Beth.

"Poor Estes," Arabella murmured.

"Yes, poor he is," the duchess said without compassion. "His legions of creditors are already pounding at his door now that his desperate financial situation is known. Henrietta is all but penniless, too, and cannot help him. The marriage settlement made no provision for her other than that she would retain full control of her then-great fortune. But she lacked her mother's shrewdness in managing it, and it dwindled away over the years, much of it to pay her son's debts."

Arabella stood up and went to the window to see whose carriage had stopped in front. To her surprise, she saw a splendid equipage, all ebony, lacquer, and brass, drawn by two matched grays. She did not recognize it or its owner whose beaver hat shadowed his face as he climbed the steps of the Vaughn residence.

"Henrietta is reaping her just reward," the duchess was saying. "She worked so hard to alienate Estes and his father, never letting them see each other when the boy was growing up."

Arabella turned away from the window, thinking of all the shocking stories that she had heard in recent days about Damon Howard. A bored society, having been tossed a scandalous new bone in the form of that hellborn bastard, had been gnawing on it ceaselessly since. By all accounts, Damon was a regular fire eater who didn't know the meaning of the word fear. He was a bruising rider, superb gambler, crack shot, and just as good with his fists as his pistols. He had won so many duels that no one dared call him out.

Arabella returned to her seat beside her aunt, complaining, "I am so tired of hearing nothing but Damon Howard talked about that I have begun to dread going out."

"I know." The duchess was amused. "They make it sound as though he successfully dueled half the bucks in England and bedded a quarter of the ladies."

Arabella's disapproval was stamped on her face. "Lady

Vaughn says that Woodthorpe doted on Damon because his behavior was even more scandalous than the earl's own."

"Damon was a hellion when he was younger," the duchess said, "But he settled down in recent years. He is said to have even a better head for financial dealings than his father, who came to rely heavily on his judgment. My solicitor says Damon was as much responsible over the years as his father for the earl's enormous fortune."

Estes had said that, too. No doubt Damon did deserve part of the earl's estate, but the stories that Arabella had heard about him had also earned him her lively dislike. "Estes says Damon is a mannerless brute."

The duchess frowned. "I cannot imagine any son of Nell Fitzhugh's being that."

Neither could Arabella. She vaguely remembered having seen Damon at Willow Wood when she was very small, but the memory was hopelessly blurred by the mists of time.

The voice of Tynes, the butler, was heard in the hall outside the withdrawing room: "Lord Vaughn will see you in the library." Tynes must be addressing the man in the beaver hat, Arabella thought.

"Now that Damon is so rich," the duchess was saying, "perhaps he can make a marriage brilliant enough to win him a place in society. By the way, did you know that the earl is so much recovered that he and Damon have gone to Willow Wood?"

Arabella's eyes widened in surprise. "But the earl has not set foot in that house since Nell died there! Why would he go now?"

The duchess shrugged. "Who knows?" She rose from the divan. "I must go before Lady Vaughn returns. How fortunate that I called while she was shopping."

As the duchess walked to the door, Arabella said hesitantly, "Aunt Margaret, you seem to know everyone in London. Do you know a man named Howard Smith?"

"Never heard of him," the duchess said briskly, going into the hall. "Who is he?"

Arabella blushed. "I don't exactly know, but he . . . he was very kind to Brom."

Her brother had made numerous inquiries about his benefactor but had learned nothing. Unfortunately, Brom had known none of the other gamblers at Getz's that night, and he dared not go back there to inquire. Arabella was as disappointed as Brom that his efforts to unearth information were fruitless.

"Speaking of your brother," the duchess said, "I hear he has finally come to his senses about that cyprian he was wild over."

"Yes. It was Mr. Smith who made him see her for what she was."

"Then we owe him a debt of gratitude, but I cannot imagine who he can be," the duchess said as Tynes opened the front door for her.

The duchess had been gone only a few minutes when Lord Estes's arrival was announced to Arabella.

As he appeared in the door of the withdrawing room, Arabella hurried toward him, then stopped. She was much startled by his appearance, upon which he normally lavished so much loving attention. He looked positively slovenly. His cravat was carelessly tied, his coat wrinkled and unbrushed, his hair oily and unkempt, and his face seemed to have aged ten years since last she had seen him.

"Please, sit down," she said weakly, gesturing toward the divan recently vacated by the duchess.

"No. Can only stay a moment." His words were slightly slurred, and he swayed unsteadily.

He is drunk, and it is not yet noon! Arabella thought.

"I must withdraw my offer to you," Lord Estes said. "Can no longer afford you. Sharks are after my flesh. Thanks to the devil who sired me, I must find a rich wife."

Happiness surged over Arabella, and she had to fight to keep her relief at being rid of him from showing on her face.

"Very sorry, Arabella. I know how much you adore me."

Her eyes widened in disbelief, then she had to bite her lips to keep from laughing. Poor Estes was a master of self-deception.

"Perhaps someday you will get over me," Estes said as he turned and, staggering slightly, stumbled out of the room.

Arabella sank down upon the sofa. Her first thought was of Beth and Justin. How could Arabella ever help the young lovers now? But that was the only regret she felt over the breaking off of her betrothal.

Voices sounded in the entry hall, and Lady Vaughn burst in upon Arabella, demanding in a querulous voice, "Have you displeased Lord Estes? We met him as he was leaving, and he barely acknowledged me. I am such a favorite of his that I know he would not act like that to me unless you had said something to affront him."

"He is no longer my betrothed."

"Oh, Arabella," Beth cried in concern, but her soft voice was drowned by her stepmother's shriek. "You wretched hoyden. What did you say to so disgust him?"

Arabella was so angered by Lady Vaughn's assumption that her stepdaughter was to blame that she forgot herself and responded tartly, "I said nothing to him. He can no longer afford a woman whose family's fortune was squandered by her extravagant stepmother."

Lady Vaughn turned lobster-red and gave Arabella a stinging slap across the face. "You ugly, disrespectful chit." She broke off at the sound of voices in the hall and hurried out to see who her husband's visitor was.

Lord Whittleson was standing there, his beaver hat already upon his head. The triumphant smile on his harsh, dissipated face only served to accentuate the whitened scar that ran diagonally from his mouth across his jaw.

Lord Vaughn was standing behind him with a sheaf of papers in his hand. Not since the day her mama had died had Arabella seen her father look so stricken.

"Lord Whittleson, what a pleasant surprise," Lady Vaughn gushed when she recognized the visitor.

"I think not," he said coldly, giving her a scathing look that bespoke louder than words what a fool he thought her. He brushed past her and disappeared through the front door.

Lady Vaughn turned with bristling indignation upon her husband. "How can you permit him to treat your wife so rudely?"

Arabella rushed up to her father. "Papa, what is the matter! You are so white and drawn. And what are those papers in your hand?"

He shook his head like a man in deep shock, brushed past Arabella, and approached his wife. "They are Lady Vaughn's bills that Lord Whittleson has bought up." He held up the papers and shook them furiously in his wife's face. "What are these? I ordered that you squander no more money that I did not have."

His wife pouted. "They were for necessities," she insisted defiantly.

"Necessities!" He read from the top paper in his hand. "Two hundred guineas for a green silk gown, fifty guineas for a bonnet." He waved the stack at her. "And they are all for similar nonsense. I hope you shall enjoy wearing your foolish, expensive finery in debtors' prison."

"You joke!"

"Oh, no, m'lady. You have provided Lord Whittleson with his long-awaited opportunity for revenge on me." He glared at her. "I also forbade you to gamble anymore."

Lady Vaughn tossed her head defiantly. "It has only been a few shillings here and there."

"Hundreds of pounds everywhere!" her husband exploded. "Whittleson has bought up your notes of hand as well as all the other debts—and the sum is so staggering that I cannot even conceive of it. Unless he is paid in full by the first of next month, which of course he cannot be, he will have me clapped into debtors' prison."

"No," Lady Vaughn shrieked, "that need not happen. Rufus Dobbs will pay any price I name to marry Beth."

Beth gave a low moan. "No, oh, please no, not that horrid man. Oh, Papa, no!"

"She *must* marry him," Lady Vaughn insisted.

Seeing the desperate look on Beth's face, Lord Vaughn said wanly, "Don't fret, Beth. I will find another way to pay my debts."

His voice lacked conviction, and Arabella swallowed hard. Her father might hold out even until the prison gates clanged shut upon him. But she knew that the dreadful life that awaited him there would soon make him agree to almost anything.

"What shall you do, Papa?" Beth asked in a despairing voice.

"I shall put this house, all its furnishings, and every other asset that I can lay my hands on except Lindley Park, which I pray I shall be able to save, up for sale. You all will return there immediately. We cannot afford the expense of two houses."

"Return to Lindley Park in midseason!" Lady Vaughn cried in dismay. "We cannot! Everyone would know the reason why. Oh, I can hear the talk now." Her voice turned coy and wheedling. "Oh, my lord, how can you be so cruel to me?"

Her beleaguered husband was unmoved. "You shall be more humiliated if I am imprisoned."

She stamped her foot angrily. "I shall not leave London."

He looked upon her with eyes so full of loathing that even she was startled into silence. "Stay, but you will not do so at my expense. Frankly, I should be greatly relieved to be rid of you.''

''Oh, oh,'' she wailed, ''how can you speak to me so cruelly? I shall have a spasm.'' Sobbing, she turned and ran up the stairs. At the top, she glanced surreptitiously around to see if her husband was following her. When she saw he was not, she ran into her apartment and slammed the door hard behind her.

Lord Vaughn said curtly to Arabella, ''See to the packing at once. *She*''—he cast a fulminating glance up the stairs— ''will never do so. I want you on your way to Lindley Park no later than the day after tomorrow. Brom will go with you while I remain here in London to try to raise money.''

Arabella nodded. As she turned away, she was struck by a thought that depressed her even further. Once gone from London, she would never see her mysterious stranger again.

Chapter 12

Two days later, Lady Vaughn and her two stepdaughters were in a carriage departing London for Lindley Park. Brom, to escape his stepmother's incessant complaining, was accompanying the women on horseback instead of riding in the coach.

Arabella, who had overseen the packing for the move while her stepmother had lain abed bewailing the cruelty of her husband, sat in one corner of the carriage. As it moved through the streets of London, Arabella searched the passersby for a tall, broad-shouldered man in elegantly tailored clothes.

The more she tried to put the midnight stranger from her mind, the more he haunted her. When she closed her eyes, she would see his extraordinary velvet brown eyes, by turn laughing, tender, concerned.

When she thought of his kiss, a glowing warmth filled her. It shocked her to realize that she longed to again feel his lips upon her own. Having been raised in strictest propriety and ignorance, Arabella was perplexed—and a little frightened—by the strange yearnings that now buffeted her.

Leaving London meant that she would have no chance of seeing him again. She tried to cheer herself by thinking how nice it would be at Lindley Park. Arabella could enjoy long rides and talks with Sally Cromwell again. Sally, who was as frank and full of fun as Arabella, had moved to Kent from Sussex only fourteen months ago upon her marriage to Benjamin Cromwell. But she and Arabella had quickly recognized in each other kindred souls and had become fast friends.

Arabella stared out the coach window at Brom, who had been as reluctant as his stepmother to leave London, complaining vehemently that the country would be so boring.

On the seat across from Arabella, Lady Vaughn was carrying on about her unfeeling husband. By forcing her to return to Lindley Park before the end of the London season, he was making her miss a number of parties that she had most particularly wished to attend.

"He knows I must go as he orders because I have no means of my own," she complained, "but I will never permit this to happen again. Next time I will be able to tell him to go to the devil." Arabella, remembering the conversation that she had overheard between Rufus Dobbs and her stepmother, knew very well how Lady Vaughn planned to obtain such means. Arabella closed her eyes. How on earth could she save Beth now?

Lady Vaughn launched into a litany of wrongs that had been done her. Included was Arabella's broken betrothal to Lord Estes. Lady Vaughn had been so eager to boast to her country neighbors of her great triumph in arranging such a brilliant match for her stepdaughter. That the match that Lady Vaughn had worked so hard to achieve had come to naught was all the fault of that despicable by-blow Damon Howard. He had turned the earl against his legitimate son and stolen poor Estes's estate from him.

In a display of illogical reasoning that quite dazzled Arabella, Lady Vaughn further insisted that it was Damon Howard's fault, too, that her husband stood at the gate of debtors' prison. Had that by-blow not cheated dear Estes out of his fortune, His Lordship would surely have paid his prospective father-in-law's debts.

Arabella, who had learned from her father the staggering size of these debts, listened to her stepmother in disbelief. Lady Vaughn was mad to think that Estes would ever have given Papa such an enormous sum.

Most aggravating of all to Lady Vaughn was the knowledge that everyone within fifty miles of Lindley Park would talk of nothing else but the Vaughns' early return there and what was behind it. She launched into a bitter diatribe about how much this would delight her bosom-bow, Mrs. Berrey, who was monstrously jealous.

Lady Vaughn and Mrs. Berrey had grown up together, and as nearly as Arabella could tell, their long friendship seemed to be rooted in mutual spite. Each loved nothing better than an opportunity to discomfort the other.

Convinced that the Vaughns' financial plight would be the sole topic of conversation at every visit, dinner, or assembly, Lady Vaughn did not know how she was to endure so much humiliation. And it was all the fault of that archdevil Damon Howard. He was her scapegoat, and as the miles dragged by, she grew increasingly vituperative about him.

By the time the carriage reached Lindley Park, Arabella cordially hoped that she would never hear Damon Howard's name again.

Contrary to Lady Vaughn's expectations, the early return to Lindley Park elicited little attention. For this, ironically, she had Damon Howard to thank.

The earl of Woodthorpe's announcement about Damon and Estes had caused, if possible, an even greater sensation in the Kent countryside surrounding Lindley Park than it had in London. It, coupled with the return of father and son to Willow Wood to reopen it for the first time since Nell Fitzhugh's death there fourteen years earlier, had left the countryside agog. No one could talk of anything but Damon Howard.

Older residents recalled when Damon had lived at Willow Wood with *that woman*. The son was remembered with no more kindness than his mother. Not only had he been a bastard, but worse still, he had been far too proud and toplofty for one born on the wrong side of the sheets. A man must know his place, and Damon Howard had had a hard time learning his. Refusing to acknowledge his own inferiority, he had challenged whoever dared to reflect poorly on his mother or himself, winning countless fisticuffs and a number of duels.

He had been a wild 'un who seemed to have sown a countryside full of wild oats. Arabella, who had been appalled by the stories that she had heard about him in London, was now treated to a seemingly endless new supply.

Then there was the delicate question of how to treat him. Over the years, the earl had purchased several properties adjacent to Willow Wood. By signing his estates over to Damon, he had made his son the largest landowner in the area. A few neighbors of practical bent pointed out that it would be deucedly awkward to ignore the richest landowner in the shire.

But the majority, who were also the most vocal, believed that the son ought to be cut as his mother had been before him. These defenders of propriety insisted that under no circumstances would they—nor should anyone—lower themselves to acknowledge him should he have the audacity to speak to them.

Lady Vaughn quickly and decisively established herself as the leader of the anti-Howard forces. Indeed, she attacked him with such fury upon the slightest opportunity that Arabella began to wonder whether Her Ladyship was not motivated by a desire to keep the neighborhood's attention so fully focused on him that it had no time to speculate on the Vaughns' situation.

The subject of all this consternation, however, seemed to

be no more interested in joining the society about him than most of its members were in having him do so. Damon Howard paid no calls, issued no invitations, and, as far as anyone could tell, never left Willow Wood.

This isolation fostered the liveliest curiosity among the ladies of the neighborhood about his appearance. He was reported to be a huge hulk of a man with the brutish build of a plow ox and a dark swarthy face that was ugly as sin. Furthermore, he was a clumsy boor without grace, style, or manners.

Arabella had no interest in the speculation about him. She was preoccupied with worry over Beth and her father. There was no word from Papa. A few days after their return to Lindley Park, Beth received a letter from Justin. He swore again his undying love for her but wrote that his conscience required him to tell her that because of his poverty, he had no hope that they could marry. The letter devastated Beth, leaving her sad and dispirited.

Two weeks after the Vaughns' return to Lindley Park, they dined at Squire Mobley's. Arabella was delighted to see that Sally Cromwell and her husband, Benjamin, were among the squire's dozen guests. The Cromwells had returned only the previous day from a three-week trip to Sussex to visit her family there. So this was the first time since Arabella had come back from London that she had seen Sally.

At the dinner table, the conversation inevitably turned to Damon Howard. Lady Vaughn quickly launched a violent verbal attack upon the presumptuous clod.

When she was done, Ben Cromwell said coldly, ''You cannot ever have met Damon. His character, manners, and dress cannot be faulted in any way. You do him a grave injustice spreading such nonsense about him.''

Silence engulfed the room. It was the first time that Arabella had ever heard anyone speak well of Damon Howard, and she was as startled as the rest of the company.

Recovering from her surprise, Lady Vaughn said hotly, "It is you who speak nonsense. He grew up here, and the stories they tell about him!"

"I have heard those stories," Sally said thoughtfully, "and none seemed truly bad to me. Most of them involved high-spirited mischief that would have been ignored had he been the earl's legitimate son. One or two were even heroic. What of the time he jumped into a frigid pond to pull out a little girl and her brother who had fallen through the ice? They would have perished had it not been for him."

"I suppose it was courageous of him to set upon young Lord Thomley, who had done nothing to him, and thrash him half to death," Lady Vaughn snapped.

"Damon caught Thomley trying to rape a village girl," Cromwell replied.

A silence fell over the table. After a moment, it was broken by Lady Vaughn. "Howard was sent down from Oxford for his wild behavior."

"I knew him at Oxford, and I admired his courage there," Cromwell said firmly. "He would permit no one to insult either his birth or his mother without being called to account."

Sally took up his defense. "Longbridge, the Sussex estate where Damon and the earl have lived in recent years, is near my parents' home. Damon was well liked and accepted in Sussex. Ben and I feel fortunate to count ourselves among his friends."

Lady Vaughn's bosom-bow, Mrs. Berrey, said in scandalized tones, "I am shocked that your husband would permit you in his company. I understand he has an insatiable eye for women."

"It is the women who have an insatiable eye for him," Sally replied. "He is exceedingly handsome."

"That is shocking beyond belief," Lady Vaughn cried, conveniently ignoring all the stories that she had heard about his conquests in London. "I cannot believe that a woman of any breeding would so lower herself."

"You have not met Damon," Sally said with a smile.

"Most fortunately I have not, and I pray I may never be subjected to such an unpleasant experience. I believe in calling a spade a spade, and I will not scruple to call him what he is, a bastard."

"You would be foolish to do so," Cromwell warned her.

When the women had left the men to their brandy and retired to the withdrawing room, Sally drew Arabella aside and asked, "Will you spend the afternoon with me tomorrow? I want a chance to hear about London without that disagreeable woman about." Sally nodded her head in the direction of Lady Vaughn, who was gossiping with Mrs. Berrey. "Please say you will come."

Arabella's eyes brightened at the prospect of spending a pleasant afternoon with Sally. "I should love to come."

"But you must promise me that you will leave your dreadful stepmother at home. I will not have her. Promise?"

Arabella, startled by how serious Sally's face was, promised.

"Good!" Sally's eyes sparkled mischievously. "I have something to show you. I think you will be very surprised."

"What is it?"

"Oh, I cannot tell you. That would spoil the fun. But remember your promise: Do not under any circumstance bring your stepmother."

But when Arabella prepared to leave for Sally Cromwell's the next day, Lady Vaughn announced that she and Beth would go, too.

Horrified, Arabella tried in vain to dissuade her stepmother. Finally Arabella said in desperation, "But Sally expressly invited only me, not you."

"Nonsense," replied Her Ladyship. "The inconsequential chit will be honored that Lady Vaughn has deigned to pay her a call.''

They were interrupted by the unexpected arrival of Lord Vaughn, looking shockingly worn and ill. The despair on his face told Arabella without words that he had failed to raise the money he needed to escape debtors' prison. It seemed to her that he had aged twenty years since they had left him a fortnight ago in London.

His wife gave him a disdainful look and headed toward the door, saying, ''Come, girls, we must be on our way to Mrs. Cromwell's.''

''We cannot go now, when Papa has just returned,'' Arabella cried. ''We must hear what he has to say.''

''Any fool can see that he has failed,'' his wife snapped.

''I will not go!'' Arabella cried, desperate to end the expedition.

''Stay,'' Lady Vaughn said. ''Beth and I shall go. Come, Beth.''

Beth cast a despairing look at Arabella and followed her stepmother out the door.

When the door closed behind them, Lord Vaughn said wearily, ''Will you sit with me for a while in the library, Arabella?''

It was the first time that she could remember his requesting her company. They walked together into the book-lined room, where he gave her an accounting of what had transpired in London.

Neither the London house nor the other assets he had sold had realized nearly so much as he had thought they would. He was far short of the amount he needed to pay off the notes that Whittleson held, and the deadline was only three days away.

''Whittleson has informed me he will be here promptly on that date with the sheriff to seize me and Lindley Park,'' Lord Vaughn said, his chin trembling.

Arabella clasped his hands, as cold as an Arctic night, with her own. "No, Papa, no!"

He whimpered. "Oh, Arabella, I cannot bear to think of what my life there will be like. Perhaps I shall be lucky, and the jail fever will carry me off immediately."

"Papa, don't talk so," she begged. But she knew that he was right. Prisons were human cesspools, reeking with filth, starvation, cruelty, and disease, and the lucky ones escaped by dying quickly. Her comfort-loving father, so indolent and weak, might well go mad if he did not die quickly.

"I imagine," he continued bitterly, "that the news I haven't a feather to fly with has been the talk of the neighborhood."

"No, the earl of Woodthorpe and his son Damon have come back to Willow Wood, and the countryside can talk of nothing else."

"What a rich man Damon is now," her father said thoughtfully. "I am so tired, Arabella, I believe I shall go up to my room for a nap. If I am lucky, Lady Vaughn will not return before dark."

But he was not lucky. Less than an hour passed before she and Beth were back. Arabella, who was still sitting in the library, hurried into the hall in time to see Lady Vaughn pick up a letter that had come for her in the day's post.

She whirled on Arabella. "Who is Sally's lover?"

Arabella looked at her blankly. "What are you talking about?"

"Your friend has an exceedingly handsome lover," she replied, going into a small sitting room with her letter and closing the door.

Arabella turned in bewilderment to her sister.

"When we arrived at Sally's, she was with a man in the drawing room," Beth explained. "As soon as we were announced, Sally rushed out and took us into a little sitting room. She seemed very startled to see us and very flustered.

In fact, she looked green. A minute or two later, the man sneaked out a side door and rode away. Only then did Sally take us into the drawing room. Clearly, she had not wanted us to see or meet the man. When Lady Vaughn demanded to know who he was, Sally told her it was none of her business. Lady Vaughn was so furious that we left immediately.''

''Did you recognize him?'' Arabella asked.

Beth shook her head. ''Neither Lady Vaughn nor I did. She insists that there can be only one reason for Sally's secretiveness. The man is her lover. Why else would Sally try to hide him and his identity?''

It was a question that Arabella could not answer. But she was shocked that her friend would be unfaithful to her husband, with whom she had seemed much in love.

Their father came down the stairs. Beth went up to him and took his hands. ''Dearest Papa, you look so tired and worn.''

He clutched her hands. Beth, with her beauty that was the picture of her late mama's and her sweet, biddable temperament, was his favorite child. ''Oh, Beth, it shall be so hard to leave you when I am cast into debtors' prison.''

''Oh, no, Papa!'' she cried in distress. ''Surely that will not happen.''

''Whether it will happen or not is up to you, Beth.'' Lady Vaughn's loud announcement from the doorway of the sitting room caused father and daughters to turn in surprise. She held up the letter she had just received. ''Rufus Dobbs again offers to pay your debts in exchange for Beth's hand in marriage.''

''Oh, no,'' Beth whimpered, turning ashen.

''Selfish chit!'' her stepmother snapped. ''Do you prefer your father to rot in debtors' prison?''

Beth's eyes flooded with tears. ''No, no, of course not.''

''It is the only way to save him,'' Lady Vaughn insisted. ''The only way.''

Beth bowed her head, and her slender frame trembled violently. "Then I shall do it," she said.

"Papa, no, don't let her," Arabella pleaded. "It will kill her; you know it will!"

"No, I must do it," Beth said with quiet determination. "I will do anything to save Papa, even marry Mr. Dobbs." Her voice broke and she began to weep.

"Dearest Beth," her father said, gathering her in his arms. "Don't cry yet. I thought of one other possibility this afternoon. I shall pursue it on the morrow."

"Fool!" his wife hissed at him. "There is no other way. Beth must marry Rufus Dobbs."

Chapter 13

When Arabella entered Beth's bedroom the next morning, she was much alarmed to find her sister pale and feverish, with eyes red from crying. But Beth was as determined as she had been the night before that if marrying Dobbs was the only way to save Papa, she would do it.

"You know how wretched the prisons are," Beth said in a weak, tremulous voice. "I cannot condemn Papa to that. I could not live with myself knowing that I was the cause of his being there."

"But you are not the cause!" Arabella protested, desperate to dissuade Beth from agreeing to a marriage that would be her death. "It is Lady Vaughn's gambling and wild extravagances that are the cause."

"I cannot let Papa go to prison," Beth said stubbornly.

"What of Justin?"

Beth's face crumpled in despair. "I shall love him till I die, but he sees no hope that we can ever marry. If I cannot marry him, what does anything matter?" Her voice faded, then recovered, and she said with more steel than Arabella had thought her delicate sister possessed, "At least this way I will save Papa."

Knowing how repulsive Beth found Dobbs, Arabella was

filled with admiration for her sweet, gentle sister's courage. Had Arabella been Dobbs's choice, she would have had to be bound hand and foot and dragged to the altar. If only Papa could find another way, any other way at all, to clear his debts.

Arabella had seen him ride off on horseback early this morning, apparently to pursue the last possibility he had mentioned yesterday. She could not imagine what it could be, but she prayed that he would meet with success.

Lord Vaughn was gone three hours. When he returned, he summoned Arabella to him in the library.

As she entered the book-lined room, she saw that his expression was the one he always wore when he was required to do something that was difficult or distasteful for him. Arabella's hopes that Beth might be spared from marriage to Dobbs crumpled.

"Shut the door," her father told her, "and sit here." He gestured at a chair facing the one in which he sat.

Obediently she closed the door and took the seat. "I fear that your mission this morning was not successful." Tears glistened in Arabella's eyes as she thought of her poor sister. "Is . . . is Beth condemned to marry Mr. Dobbs?"

"That is for you to decide, Arabella. Your sister's fate now rests in your hands."

"What!" Arabella gasped. "You know I will do anything to save Beth from Dobbs. What must I do?"

"I have received an offer to pay all of our debts. I will even be permitted to retain title to the house and some of the land here at Lindley Park, which is more than I had hoped for." As he talked, Arabella saw that the flat despair to which he had been prisoner had been replaced by hope. "I would be saved from debtors' prison. We all would be spared enormous humiliation, and the Vaughns would still own Lindley Park as they have for two centuries. Brom would have an inheritance. But most important of all, your sister will not have to marry that stinking pig Dobbs. It is an incredibly generous offer, and I cannot tell you how grateful I am for it. All that remains is for you to agree to it.''

''But what have I to agree to?''

''To marry Damon Howard.''

Arabella turned quite as white as the lace edging the neckline of her blue cotton morning gown. She could not have been more stunned had her father asked her to marry the devil himself. In fact, given Damon's reputation, Arabella could not see much difference. The deep pride in her lineage that had been so carefully inculcated in her over the years rose up in revolt at the thought of such a degrading mesalliance with a baseborn stranger. ''The *bastard!*'' she cried.

''Do not ever call him that to his face,'' her father said sternly. ''He is a proud man, and he would never forgive you.''

''What has he to be proud of?'' Arabella demanded angrily, remembering all the shocking stories she had heard about him. By most accounts, he was at least as ugly and disgusting a specimen as Rufus Dobbs, if not worse. Even his own half brother had called him a crude, stupid brute. Arabella's blood ran cold at the thought of spending her life with a man deficient in intelligence, sensibility, appearance, and manners.

''I warn you, Arabella,'' her papa said, ''he is not a man to be toyed with. You will do well to try to fix his interest, not disgust him.''

''Surely you cannot expect me to marry such a man. I do not even know him. And why would he want to marry me, a stranger?''

''He doesn't want to.''

Arabella's mind reeled. ''What!''

''He doesn't want to marry you. Another reason why you

must try very hard to fix his interest. It is his father who wishes the marriage.''

Arabella stared with stricken eyes at her father. All of her other objections to such an unsuitable match paled before the information that Damon Howard no more wanted her than she did him.

Lord Vaughn was saying, ''I had heard that Woodthorpe wanted desperately to marry Damon well enough to provide him entry into society. That is why I went to see the earl this morning.''

''You went to the earl and offered me to his bastard in return for payment of your debts?'' Arabella was so humiliated that her father had initiated this bargain that she could not manage to raise her voice above a whisper.

''I did,'' her father confirmed, oblivious to Arabella's shame. ''Woodthorpe was very receptive to the idea.''

''But his son was not?''

''No, Damon was quite opposed to it at first.''

The room spun before Arabella's eyes. The humiliation of having been bartered to a disreputable, ugly by-blow who did not even want her was so devastating that she felt as though she would die from shame. ''What were his objections?'' she demanded in a seething voice.

''He asked whether you wished the match,'' her father said. ''When I told him that you knew nothing of it yet, he said that he wanted no part of an unwilling bride.''

''What made him come round?'' Arabella's voice was laced with bitterness. ''His great hunger for social position?''

''Partly, I suppose, but I think it was more because his father so fervently wished it. It is clear that Damon would do almost anything to make Woodthorpe happy.''

''Of course he would!'' Arabella's shame spawned an irrational fury. ''No doubt that is how he convinced the earl to give him his great fortune and leave poor Lord Estes out in the cold!"

Lord Vaughn ignored her interruption. "Damon and the earl had a long talk in private while I waited. After it, Damon reluctantly agreed to the match provided that your aunt the duchess of Hampshire will agree to your being married under her aegis."

Arabella was infuriated by the gall of this stipulation. Of course it would help assure him of social acceptance, but to demand it as a condition of marrying her was insufferable. "I cannot marry such a disgusting man!" she exploded.

"He is not disgusting. Besides, it is nothing but a marriage of convenience for both of you. Under such circumstances, I doubt that he will be a very demanding husband."

Arabella, in her innocence, wondered what her father meant by demanding.

"From what I hear," her father continued, "he has no trouble finding women to amuse him."

Arabella's face reddened. Would Damon abandon her as his father had abandoned his countess? "How can you marry me to such a man?"

Her father seemed surprised by her outburst. "I think he is good and generous."

"*Good!* You cannot have heard the evil stories they tell about him."

"But I know how generous he has been to me," Lord Vaughn said patiently. "It was he who said I should be allowed to keep some of Lindley Park. He even offered to help me restore it to profitability. At least reserve judgment of him until you have met. He will call upon you tomorrow."

"How eager he is to meet his bride!" Arabella's words dripped with sarcasm.

"You do him an injustice. He strongly desired to come

back with me today to see you, but I insisted that he must wait until tomorrow. I know your impetuous frankness, and I wanted to give you time to get over your . . . uh . . . surprise. By the way, Damon said he would bring you a betrothal present that he thinks will please you greatly.''

His presumption further infuriated Arabella. ''What effrontery for a man who does not know me to say such a thing! No doubt it is some trumpery jewels. Tell him that I do not like jewels and he may keep them!''

''Do not act like that,'' her father pleaded. ''I warn you again: You would be a fool not to strive to fix his interest.''

''You offered me for sale, Papa, to a social outcast, and he deigned to accept me. I have no wish to fix his interest and even less to marry him!''

''Do you refuse?''

Arabella tossed her head defiantly. ''If I do?''

''Beth will have to marry Dobbs.''

''No,'' Arabella cried, suddenly hating herself. She remembered how courageous Beth had been, insisting upon sacrificing herself to that hideous Dobbs to save Papa. What a selfish coward Arabella was next to her sister. And what of Arabella's vow that she would save Beth and thwart Lady Vaughn's scheming with Dobbs?

In a voice choked with conflicting emotions, Arabella said, ''I will do anything to prevent Beth's having to marry Dobbs.'' She slumped dejectedly down in her chair and conceded in a whisper, ''I will marry Damon Howard.''

To Arabella, who had never felt more humiliated and wretched in her life, the happiness on her father's face was nearly unbearable.

The door of the library was flung open, and Lady Vaughn swept in. Instantly the happiness faded from her husband's face. ''Do you not know how to knock, madam?''

She ignored his irritable question and informed him, ''I am writing Mr. Dobbs that we accept his offer.''

Lord Vaughn half started up out of his chair in anger. "You will do nothing of the sort. Beth will not marry Mr. Dobbs. I forbid it."

Lady Vaughn was taken aback by her husband's anger, but she said contemptuously, "You may prefer to rot in debtors' prison, but what of your responsibility to your family? Are we to starve so you may protect your precious daughter's selfish wishes?"

"No, it is Arabella who will marry to save me."

"You fool," his wife hissed. "Mr. Dobbs had no interest in that ill-behaved chit. It is Beth he desires."

"Tell Mr. Dobbs to go to the devil. He will marry no daughter of mine. A gentleman has agreed to pay my debts in exchange for Arabella's hand."

"Who is the fool!" Lady Vaughn demanded.

"Damon Howard."

Lady Vaughn turned ashen. "You are surely joking. He is a bastard and a scoundrel. You cannot permit Arabella to marry so far beneath herself."

"He is not so far beneath us as Dobbs," her husband said. "And it is settled. She will marry Howard."

"That ugly brute is what the chit deserves, but I will not permit it." Lady Vaughn's face was working convulsively, and Arabella could almost read her mind. Her stepmother could not bear that the man whom she had loudly proclaimed so far beneath her that she would never deign to speak to him would be her son-in-law. With what glee her bosom-bow Mrs. Berrey would relentlessly remind her.

"I will not have that bastard in my family," Lady Vaughn cried.

"Your extravagances have left us no choice," her husband said coldly.

His wife's face was livid. She turned and stalked from the library, muttering, "I *will* prevent such a humiliating match."

For once Arabella hoped that Lady Vaughn would succeed.

But not at Beth's expense.

Chapter 14

When Arabella left her father in the library, she went with dragging, spiritless steps to her room, where she laid her aching head down upon her pillow and tried to sort out her angry, confused emotions.

She could not have been there more than three minutes when her stepmother stalked in without knocking. Lady Vaughn informed Arabella that since she was about to be married, it was time that she was told about a wife's conjugal duties.

Arabella, who had been raised in sheltered ignorance of this aspect of married life, was very curious. It always had been alluded to before her only in the most vague and veiled of terms, and her own imagination had woven about it golden, romantic gossamer.

These delicate strands were quickly shredded by her stepmother's graphically ugly, sadistic description of the pain and humiliation that a rutting husband inflicted upon a wife. The innocent Arabella was at first repelled, then revolted, and finally terrified at Her Ladyship's discourse on marital love in terms so brutal that her husband would have been both astounded and outraged had he been privy to them. The tortures of the inquisition paled in comparison to what a poor wife must endure to sate her husband's animal lust.

"Why does any woman marry?" Arabella gasped in horror.

Her stepmother shrugged. "It is, like childbirth, one of the agonies that are a woman's lot to endure. Of course, you will hate it. Every woman does. The most she can hope for is a gentleman of refinement who adores her, so that his love and breeding will dictate some consideration for her." Lady Vaughn shuddered. "How I pity you, poor Arabella. How much worse it will be for you."

Arabella's azure eyes were wide and frightened. "Why?"

"Damon Howard is an ugly, crude brute without breeding. The thought of what you will suffer at his hands makes me faint." Lady Vaughn passed a plump hand in front of her eyes as though trying to brush away the horror. "How very brave you are to agree to marry him."

Had Arabella's mind not been crushed by misery and shame from the cumulative blows of the day's nightmarish revelations, she would have been suspicious of her stepmother's sudden, uncharacteristic solicitude. But Arabella's nerves were already overwrought, and she was engulfed by fear and dread.

"Of course, he only wants to marry you for your social position," her stepmother assured her. "If you have any sense, you will insist upon a marriage of convenience in which it is agreed beforehand that there will be no intimacy between you."

Now Arabella grasped what her father had meant when he had talked of Damon not being too demanding. Arabella stammered in a frightened voice, "Papa said it would be—" She broke off, too distressed to continue.

"Pray to God that your papa is right!" Lady Vaughn cast her eyes dramatically heavenward as if she, too, were beseeching the Almighty on behalf of her stepdaughter. "The disgusting brute is so desperate for social acceptance that if you insist upon an unconsummated marriage before you are wed, he undoubtedly would agree to it rather than chance jeopardizing the marriage."

"Do you think so?" Arabella asked.

Lady Vaughn nodded. "Tell him to take a mistress—or several if he wishes—and leave you alone. A man doesn't care with whom he satisfies his lusts so long as they are satisfied."

Arabella was sickened by the whole discussion. "If what happens is so dreadful, why would any woman consent to be a man's mistress?"

Lady Vaughn gave a disgusted sniff. "Mistresses are well rewarded. Some women will do anything for money."

After Lady Vaughn left, Arabella lay upon her bed, a seething cauldron of emotions. She was utterly humiliated at having been sold sight unseen to a social outcast who—most unforgivable insult of all—did not even want her and would reluctantly accept her only if her illustrious aunt would sponsor the wedding. Her cheeks burned with shame.

Arabella thought of all the shocking stories that she had heard about Damon Howard. Lady Vaughn was no doubt right. Such a man, caring nothing for Arabella, would be merciless in his use of her.

It was more than Arabella could bear. Waves of nausea washed over her. When they receded, she jumped up from her bed with sudden resolve. She would marry him. It was the only way to save Beth and her father. But Lady Vaughn was right: Arabella must insist on an unconsummated marriage.

The impetuosity that had so often gotten Arabella into trouble propelled her now to the slender mahogany writing table that had once belonged to her mama. Seizing paper and pen, she began a letter. Her shame and her dread quite overwhelmed her good sense, and she vented her boiling emotions by spilling a torrent of hot, bitter words upon the page.

Yes, she wrote, she would marry him. But though he might win her hand, he would never win her heart. How could he, a baseborn bastard, be so presumptuous as to think he could win the love or even the respect of a lady of quality? And she wanted it understood from the outset that theirs would be a marriage of convenience only.

Never, never, never (underlined several times with thick, blunt strokes for added emphasis) would she willingly be intimate with such an odious ugly brute as himself. However, she was perfectly willing, indeed anxious, that he should take a mistress and spare his wife.

And have no fear, Arabella wrote, she would do everything in her power to assure him that he got what he had paid for: social standing—although it hardly seemed so important that to obtain it, a man would marry a woman whom he did not know and who found him repulsive.

Her hasty pen stopped. The fact that a man so inferior to her had to be persuaded to accept her galled her more than anything else, and she added pettishly, ''a woman who, in fact, is in love with another man.''

For, Arabella told herself, she was in love. Not with Lord Estes, certainly, but with the midnight stranger. The thought of him, of his velvet soft eyes, and of his kiss brought tears to her eyes. He was lost to her forever.

Bitterly Arabella sealed the letter. Then came the problem of whom she could get to deliver it. Brom had gone to Squire Mobley's an hour before and was not expected back until late tonight. Finally she bribed a groom to take the letter to Willow Wood. Then she had a horse saddled for herself and rode for nearly two hours across the rolling green hills.

Slowly the ride siphoned off her poisonous emotions, and she began to think more rationally. The sun was hot, and on her way back to the house, she stopped by a towering horse chestnut tree on a hillside overlooking the road from Willow Wood. She dismounted and took refuge in the shade of its spreading branches.

Now that she was thinking more clearly, she sincerely repented having written Damon so insultingly. How cruel and unfair it had been of her to do so when she had not even met him.

True, there were all the derogatory stories she had heard about him. But Sally and Ben Cromwell, whose opinions she respected, had praised him. And Damon was, as her aunt had pointed out, Nell's son. Arabella could not imagine that exquisite creature producing a monster. Her father had been right. She should have at least reserved judgment until she met Damon.

In the distance, Arabella saw a rider on the road, galloping toward her, coming from Willow Wood. She wondered if it was Damon Howard. What was he like? She tried to remember the youth that she had seen at Willow Wood when she had been a toddler, but he was lost in the faceless blur of time.

Now that her initial shock and outrage had spent itself, Arabella had accepted the inevitability of marrying him. It was the only possible way that she could save Beth from Dobbs. Furthermore, Damon was so rich that perhaps he would help Beth and Justin so that they, too, could marry. If only he would do that, Arabella would gladly marry him.

Still it would be very awkward to ask him after he had been so generous to her father—and especially after her wretched letter to him.

Now that she was resigned to marrying him, a new and chilling fear struck her. What if, after reading her angry, insulting letter, he refused to marry her? She shivered with fear as it struck her that such a letter to a man of Howard's temperament could only have infuriated and hardened him against her. If only she had not sent it.

The rider neared her, and Arabella saw that it was her father. But why was he coming from Willow Wood? Seeing her on the hillside, he left the road and galloped up to her. She rose from the grass, wondering what he wanted. When he stopped in front of her, he was angrier than she had ever seen him.

"What the devil did you mean by writing that evil letter?" he exclaimed as he dismounted. "If your aim was to give Damon a disgust of you, you succeeded beyond your wildest hopes. He is so enraged that he refuses now to marry you."

Arabella's heart seemed to sink to her feet. Oh, God, what had she done? Her father had warned her against angering Damon or calling him a bastard. In her angry humiliation, she had foolishly done both.

Her father continued with blazing eyes. "I cannot blame him in the slightest. He was so generous to us, and you thanked him with the most vile letter I have ever read."

"He let you read it?"

Her father nodded. "When Damon sent me a curt note saying that he was withdrawing his offer, I rode immediately to Willow Wood to find out why. I have never seen a man so furious. When he showed me your letter, I understood why." Lord Vaughn suddenly looked very old and tired. "There is no hope for us now but that Rufus Dobbs will have Beth."

Arabella could only stare at her father in stricken silence as she grasped the full folly of what she had done. How could she have so hurt Beth? Arabella quavered, "Is there no hope that Damon will relent?"

"I am afraid not. I told him how impetuous you are and that I had handled telling you badly. I assured him that you had written the letter in your initial shock and did not mean it, but he was adamant that he would not marry you. He does, however, demand an apology from you."

Yes, she at least owed him that, Arabella thought miserably.

"I finally persuaded him to let you apologize in person,"

her father was saying. "Damon very reluctantly said he would come to Lindley Park at five this afternoon. I am not sure that he will, but if he does, you will beg his forgiveness—on hands and knees if necessary—and assure him that you would be honored to marry him. You will agree to whatever he wants. I don't care what it is. Not that it is likely to make any difference."

Lord Vaughn's shoulders sagged in despair. "I do not believe anything will move him. Still, you must try for Beth's sake, if not for mine."

Arabella thought of Beth and bowed her head in defeat.

"Come back to the house with me so that you can be ready when—if—he comes," her father said. "You will endeavor to make yourself as lovely as possible."

At the house they were met by Lady Vaughn, who said gloatingly, "So you were clever enough, Arabella, to get the bastard to break the betrothal."

To her husband she added with a gleam of triumph in her eyes, "Now Beth will have to marry Mr. Dobbs."

It struck Arabella with the force of a slap that she had played into Lady Vaughn's scheming hands. Now her stepmother would collect the handsome reward that Dobbs had promised her. *"Some women will do anything for money,"* Lady Vaughn had said. And she was one of them!

With a sob, Arabella fled up the stairs.

Chapter 15

Arabella had never before lavished so much attention on her toilet as she did in dressing for her introduction to Damon Howard. She chose a gown of azure silk that was the identical color of her eyes. It was simply cut, with a low, rounded neck, fitted waist, and dainty capped sleeves, but its clinging silk accentuated the slender curves of her figure as its color did her eyes. She wore no jewels, only a tiny gold locket on a slender gold chain about her neck.

Masses of wavy hair were piled high atop her head like a chestnut crown, but three long curls had been allowed to escape and hung artfully down.

Arabella did not want to irritate Damon further by keeping him waiting, so she took care to be ready well before the time for his visit. She trembled at the thought of facing him. Over and over she damned her impetuosity. The searing words of her terrible letter haunted her. She would have given anything to have never written them. If only she had followed her father's advice and tried to win Damon over, instead of driving him away. Would she never learn?

She had jeopardized Beth's future—and her own—to mollify her own foolish pride. She had wanted to shame him in order to ease her own mortification. Even if Damon could somehow be persuaded to marry her now, she would never be able to get him to help Beth and Justin. Oh, what a mull she had made of it all.

She went into the drawing room to await Damon's arrival with Beth and her father. Brom was still at Squire Mobley's. Lady Vaughn had announced that under no circumstances would she condescend to welcome such a disreputable man and remained in her apartment upstairs.

As the appointed moment for his arrival approached, Arabella grew increasingly nervous. She had taken a seat on a sofa that faced away from the door and looked out over the garden, now a riot of color: Red-and-white snapdragons, blue-and-white bellflowers, golden poppies, white candytuft, and red feverfew. It was a casual garden, its borders defined by flowering shrubbery: lilacs, sun roses, and the arching wands of spireas thick with tiny white flowers. Mounds of viburnum and heather lay before their taller neighbors.

Even the serenity of the garden she so loved could not soothe Arabella's tortured nerves. She was torn between terror that Damon would not come and fear of facing him if he did.

The hands of the ebony-and-gold bracket clock on the mantel moved with maddening slowness past the appointed hour for his arrival. Arabella's index finger nervously traced the outline of a Meissen porcelain that decorated the table next to the sofa. It was a prized piece of a woman with a miniature tea set on a tray. Each tiny piece of the set was exquisite in its delicate perfection.

Another fifteen minutes crept by, and her father said bitterly, "He is not coming. You have succeeded in driving him away, Arabella. I hope you are well satisfied."

At that moment the sound of a vehicle was heard outside. Lord Vaughn jumped up and ran to the window.

"Thank God, it is he!" he exclaimed, and rushed into the

hall to greet his guest. Beth also rose and went to wait near the drawing room door. Only Arabella, who was shaking so that she dared not attempt to stand, remained seated. She could not even force herself to turn her head around toward the door, where she might catch a glimpse of Damon Howard.

She heard the low murmur of voices, then the sound of footsteps entering the drawing room. As they neared the sofa where Arabella sat, she felt as though her executioner were approaching.

Her father's voice, so obsequious and placating that it made her wince, reassured Mr. Howard that she had not meant a word of that dreadful letter and longed only for an opportunity to apologize to him in person.

Lord Vaughn's voice turned harsh. "Arabella, come here so I may present Mr. Howard to you and you may tell him how much you regret writing that letter."

With shaking limbs, Arabella rose slowly to her feet. The footsteps had stopped very near the table beside the sofa, and she knew that Damon Howard stood not more than three feet from her.

But for a long moment she could not force herself to turn around and face the stranger who was to be her destiny—or her family's destruction.

The room grew oppressively still.

"Arabella!" her father commanded angrily. Still she could not force herself to obey.

"Embarrassed to face me, Miss Vaughn?" a deeper voice demanded, adding with a note of suppressed fury, "You ought to be!"

Arabella gasped. It was the voice of the midnight stranger!

She whirled around and found herself looking at the strong, handsome face that had haunted her. Only now the deep brown eyes were so very different: no longer like velvet in their warm softness but like iron in their cold hardness.

She stared at him in unholy confusion. Her mouth formed the word "you," but no sound came from it. Her surprise was mirrored for a fleeting instant in his own. Arabella realized with sickening clarity that he thought she had surely realized by now that Howard Smith was Damon Howard. Arabella tried again to speak, but she could produce only a squeak.

Damon hastily snatched up the porcelain woman at tea from the table. "Is this Meissen?" he asked, skillfully diverting Lord Vaughn's and Beth's attention from Arabella's stunned countenance.

"Yes," Lord Vaughn said, greatly puzzled at Damon's sudden interest in porcelain at such a moment.

"What an exceptional piece," Damon said, proceeding to enumerate in detail the reasons why until Arabella could manage to control her shock. She was weak with gratitude that despite his fury at her, he was still kind enough to spare her having to explain to her father her peculiar reaction.

Damon was dressed in the first stare of elegance: a perfectly tailored blue superfine coat; a snowy, intricately tied cravat; and the black pantaloons that were all the rage in London now. How handsome he was.

When Damon saw that Arabella had recomposed herself, he replaced the porcelain on the table and said, "But I digress, Lord Vaughn. It is time that I was introduced to your daughter."

After her father completed the formal presentation, Damon said smoothly, his eyes hard and unreadable, "You are quite as lovely as your father assured me that you were."

Damon betrayed not the slightest indication that he had seen Arabella before. He was keeping his promise that if they were ever introduced, he would pretend not to know her.

Arabella stared dumbly at him, envying his coolness. Her heart was pounding with such loudness and rapidity that surely even the cook in the kitchen could hear it.

"You, sir," she faltered, "are not at all what I expected."

His eyes remained cold and hard. "I am sorry to disappoint you, Miss Vaughn, but I always leave my horns and tail at home when I pay formal calls."

Lord Vaughn hastily interjected, "Arabella certainly did not mean to imply in her letter that you were a devil."

"It was one of the nicer things she called me," Damon said sardonically. "Your daughter made it very clear that she did not want my offer. You will be happy to know, Miss Vaughn, that I have no intention of marrying you."

Looking at the hard cast of his face, Arabella recognized that he was controlling a volcanic temper with an unshatterable iciness. But within him, his anger seethed and boiled like molten lava. Such a man would not soon or easily forget the insults that she had dealt him in that letter. It was all Arabella could do to keep from bursting into tears. What cruel irony that she had been betrothed against her will to the very man she dreamed of and had succeeded in driving him away.

Lord Vaughn said, "Arabella wishes nothing so much as to marry you."

"Does she indeed?" The flat disbelief in Damon's cold voice sent a nervous chill along Arabella's spine.

"Yes, I do," she cried, looking at him beseechingly.

Damon's eyes narrowed. "I desire, Lord Vaughn, to talk to your daughter privately."

His Lordship said hastily, "I don't think that will be necessary. Arabella is perfectly willing—"

"Pardon me, Lord Vaughn," Damon interrupted, "but it is very necessary to me. In fact *crucial*."

Her father reluctantly led them to a small sitting room off the drawing room and closed the door upon them.

As soon as Arabella was alone with Damon, she faced him and cried in anguish, "If I had had any idea who you were, I would never have written that terrible letter."

The thick black triangles that were his eyebrows rose

skeptically. "You are not stupid, Miss Vaughn. My presence in the neighborhood has hardly gone unnoticed. That coupled with all that I knew about you and your family should have made it quite obvious who I was."

She hung her head. "Now that I know, I cannot understand how I could have been such a chucklehead. But I swear to you, I did not even suspect. Had I known it was you, I would never have objected to marrying you."

The triangular brows telegraphed even greater skepticism. "Even though you love another?"

Arabella blushed crimson, and her customary frankness failed her. If she confessed that he was the man she had written him of, he would believe her to be an even greater fool than he already thought her. No intelligent, well-bred woman fell in love with a man she had seen only twice and under such peculiar circumstances. Far more mortifying to her, however, was the realization that although he had known her identity, he had strenuously objected to marrying her. Her pride would not permit her to admit to a man who clearly cared nothing for her that she loved him.

She stammered evasively, "You have been so good to me, and I am so grateful to you."

"You are agreeable to marrying for gratitude instead of love, Miss Vaughn?"

His cool, sardonic voice and hard, unfriendly eyes unnerved her. Had she alienated him totally with that fatal letter? She again evaded his question, saying hastily, "I have not had a chance to thank you for what you did for Brom."

"What I did for you or him in no way changes what I am, Miss Vaughn. I am still Damon Howard, bastard and social outcast."

Only the tiniest of inflections in his cold voice betrayed how much Arabella's letter had wounded him.

She flinched as though he had slapped her. "Damon, I cannot tell you how much I regret writing that letter. My impetuosity is forever getting me into such dreadful trouble. I was sorry that I wrote it even before I knew who you were. But now . . .''

"Why, pray tell, were you sorry before?"

"Because it was so cruel and unfair of me to judge a man that I had never met."

His eyes remained so cold and hard toward her that she wondered if they would ever thaw. He seemed far more a stranger now than he had been that night on the road. Somehow she had to make him understand. "But I was so terribly shocked and so angry and humiliated—"

Fury danced in his eyes. "Humiliated at marrying a —"

Arabella impetuously clapped her hand over his mouth so that his bitter words were silenced. A tremor went through her at the touch of his mouth upon her palm, and her memory of his kiss nearly undid her.

"No," she cried, hastily removing her hand from his mouth, "humiliated because my father offered me for sale to a man who I thought had not even seen me since I was in leading strings." Tears shimmered in her eyes. "And you! You did not even want me! Papa said it took a great deal of persuasion to convince you to take me. Was I so objectionable to you?"

For the first time, his eyes softened. "No, but I had no wish to buy a bride. I preferred to court and win my own."

His words burned Arabella like hot embers, for they confirmed to her that she would not have been his own choice. He had known her identity, yet he had made no effort to see her, let alone court her. "Why did you finally agree to marry me?" she demanded bitterly. "Was it because of your father, or was it your longing for social position?"

This question seemed to startle, then anger him. His eyes flashed dangerously, but when he replied, it was in a mocking, off-handed tone. "Oh, social position, of course."

Arabella felt as though he had buried a knife in her. She

loved him, but he did not reciprocate. And she, stupid, impetuous creature that she was, had sunk herself below reproach with that horrid letter. He would use her letter as an excuse to end a betrothal he had not wanted. But now that she knew who he was, she desperately wanted it—and him. With breaking heart, she blurted, "Will you marry me?"

For the first time that day, the teasing smile that had so charmed her played on his lips. "I believe, Miss Vaughn, that I am the one who is supposed to ask that question."

She was too overwrought to respond to his dry humor. Instead, she persisted with utmost seriousness. "Will you cry off our betrothal?"

His face hardened. "I will not have a marriage in name only, as you demanded in your letter. Do you want to be my wife in every sense of the word?"

Arabella thought of Lady Vaughn's terrifying description and felt faint. To conceal her fear, she stared down at the Aubusson carpet on the floor. "I do," she said in a weak voice.

"Such enthusiasm," Damon said sarcastically. "Let me remind you that I must pay an extortionate price to marry you. I do not think I am being unreasonable to require in return that you fulfill your wifely obligation, including intimacy and fidelity."

His hand settled on her chin. His touch sent an excited shiver through her as he forced her face gently but firmly upward toward his own. His brown eyes searched her azure ones. "Are you willing to give up the man you love for me?"

"What?" Arabella asked, startled.

Damon repeated his question.

Arabella could not bring herself to risk his further censure by admitting that he was the man and that she, silly goose, had fallen in love with a stranger who did not want her. She swallowed hard and, not trusting herself to speak, nodded an assent.

His sharp brown eyes narrowed angrily. "Who is this man that you love?"

"It would be indiscreet of me to tell," she stammered.

"I do not want discretion in a wife," he snapped, releasing her chin abruptly. "I want fidelity."

Arabella met his angry gaze steadily. "I vow to you that you shall have it."

"Very well. If the duchess of Hampshire agrees to sponsor our wedding, I will marry you."

Somehow Arabella managed to conceal her pain at this blunt reminder of why he was marrying her, but her voice faltered as she asked, "What if she refuses?"

"Then we cannot marry."

Arabella felt as though he had slapped her, and she said coldly, "I shall write the duchess at once to ask her."

"I have already done so," he said.

Arabella was startled by his boldness.

He continued. "If she agrees, we shall be married in three weeks in London."

"Why so soon?" Arabella exclaimed.

"My father's health is still very fragile, and his fondest wish is for this marriage. I want it to take place as soon as possible—just in case."

The pain on Damon's face was so acute that Arabella forgot her own hurt. She longed to take him in her arms and comfort him as he had comforted her after saving her from the highwaymen.

She asked softly, "You love him very much, don't you?"

"Yes." This single word was weighted with anguish.

"I know how you feel," Arabella said, touching his arm. "I remember when Mama was dying. I loved her so much, and I wanted so desperately to drive death away. But there was nothing I could do but stand helplessly by and watch her suffer."

He put his hand over hers and smiled sadly at her. Then he

turned away from her and went to the window, where he stared silently out at the colorful display of flowers in the garden. When he turned back to her, his face had been composed into a mask that betrayed no emotion.

"I am very grateful to you for not telling anyone about our meeting on the heath," Arabella said shyly.

"I promised I would not betray you," Damon said. "I did tell my father, but your secret is safe with him."

"I am surprised he would want me for a daughter-in-law. He must have been horrified."

"Amused," Damon said. "I almost forgot to tell you about my betrothal gift to you."

"You need not give me anything," Arabella told him. "You have been far too generous already. I want nothing more."

His eyes were teasing. "Oh, I think you will want this."

"What is it?" she asked, exceedingly curious to know what he had chosen for her.

"A small but quite profitable estate that I shall deed over to Beth. I shall notify Justin that he can now afford to sell out his commission and return home to marry her."

Tears of gratitude flooded Arabella's eyes. Damon had given her what she most wanted without her even having to ask him. "You are so good and kind," she said, adding more to herself than to him, "yet people tell such dreadful stories about you."

"Especially your stepmother."

Arabella's startled look brought a wry smile to his lips. "Oh, yes, I am well aware of what Lady Vaughn—and others—say about me."

"Is none of it true?" Arabella asked hopefully.

He shrugged carelessly. "Oh, a good deal of it is. But it all happened years ago, when I was very young. People ignore the exemplary life I have led the past several years and repeat the old stories about me as though they had just happened.''

A musing expression crept across his face. ''You see, I adored my mother, and I took her death very hard. My father, thinking to distract me from my grief, sent me off to Oxford. He meant well, but it was the worst thing he could have done. At least here in Kent I was merely cut because of my birth, but there I was taunted incessantly. The other students quickly discovered how sensitive I was to anything said about my mother and subjected me to a barrage of insults about her. I challenged every man who dared utter one, and there were many who did.''

''And rued the day, too, from what I heard,'' Arabella said softly.

A wry smile twisted his lips. ''I was a nonpareil when it came to dueling and brawling. I was sent down from Oxford very quickly. Like Brom, I became rebellious, and I lived a wild life for a time in London. But after a while, I grew up.''

Arabella grimaced as she recalled aloud what her aunt had said. ''Dueling the bucks and bedding the ladies.''

Damon sighed wearily. ''Once I took a perverse pleasure in being welcomed into the beds of ladies who would not allow me to be seen in their drawing rooms. In time I tired of such hypocrisy.'' His face was harsh. ''Not a very pretty story, is it? One of the penalties of becoming notorious is that you never escape your reputation.'' He gave her a crooked smile. ''Do you still want to marry me?''

Arabella blushed and nodded.

His eyes studied her with cool appraisal. Suddenly, without warning, his hands reached up and cupped her head as his lips claimed hers in a possessive, probing kiss. She stiffened in surprise. Then as the seductive heat of his mouth warmed her, she softened. Feeling her resistance fade, he slipped his hands from around her head to wrap her in his arms. Her heart thudded with excitement, and she melted into his embrace. His kiss grew more fiery and demanding. She found herself returning it with an ardor that surprised them both.

Suddenly his mouth abandoned hers, wrenching an involuntary murmur of disappointment from her. He stared down at her silently, with a strange, speculative look.

Finally he took her arm and said, "Come, we must return to your family."

He escorted Arabella back to the drawing room, where Lady Vaughn, unable to contain her curiosity, had joined her husband and Beth. Arabella bit her lip when she saw her stepmother and prayed that she would not create a scene.

Damon's announcement that his betrothal to Arabella was reinstated brought three very different reactions: Lord Vaughn was relieved; Beth, anxious; and Lady Vaughn, furious.

"You shall not be married from Lindley Park," Her Ladyship snapped. "I will not have it."

"I refuse to be married from Lindley Park," Damon responded coolly. "We will be married in London, and I expressly prohibit you, Lady Vaughn, from attending." He turned to Lord Vaughn. "Indeed, sir, if she attempts to do so, your daughter will find herself abandoned at the altar. Do I make myself clear?"

Lord Vaughn nodded. "I promise you that she will not be there."

Lady Vaughn was so angry that for several seconds she could do no more than sputter. Finally she spit out, "You insulting coxcomb! Does it please you to buy as your wife a woman who loves your half brother, Lord Estes?"

At the mention of Arabella's former betrothed, Damon's eyes kindled with intense hatred and the color drained from his face. Damon clearly loathed his half brother. Was it because Lord Estes would be an earl, or because he was legitimate?

Damon wheeled on Arabella with furious eyes. "Is that true? Estes is the man you love?"

"Of course it is true," Lady Vaughn assured him before Arabella could speak. "They were secretly betrothed."

Damon regarded Arabella with disgust. "How could you? Who broke off the betrothal?"

"He did," Arabella began miserably, longing to strangle Lady Vaughn's evil tongue into silence. "But—"

Lady Vaughn rudely interrupted Arabella. "When you turned your father against Lord Estes and robbed him of his rightful fortune, he was forced to seek a rich bride. Poor Arabella was heartbroken."

Arabella started to protest her stepmother's lie, but Damon gave her a look so scathing that her words died in her throat. His lips curled contemptuously. "At least you were honest enough to write me that you loved another."

Arabella cursed that fatal letter. Would its repercussions never end?

Damon's words were like icicles cracking: "You might have carried your honesty a step farther, however, and informed me that my half brother was your great love."

Never had Arabella felt so trapped. If only she had confessed the truth to Damon when they had been in the sitting room. She could not tell him now before her family, especially Lady Vaughn, for she could not explain how she had met him.

Arabella took Damon's arm and tried to guide him back to the little sitting room. "If we could talk privately, I can explain."

He jerked away from her. "We have already talked privately, and you unwittingly explained a good deal more than you intended. No wonder you would not tell me the identity of your lover."

"Lord Estes is not my lover," Arabella cried desperately.

Damon's face twisted into a bitter sneer. "Let me correct myself: the man you love."

"I swear to you, Damon, that I want to marry you, not Lord Estes."

"How touching." Damon's words dripped with sarcasm. His brown eyes were furious. "Since Lord Estes can no longer afford to marry you, you let your father convince you that you should settle for the Howard fortune instead."

His unjust accusation kindled her own temper, and in her anger she cried, "What of you? You did not want to marry me! *You* let *your* father convince you that you should settle for me because it would give you the social position you so desperately want!"

He stared at her blankly, as though she were talking gibberish.

"Do you deny that you told me so?" Arabella cried, tears welling in her eyes.

"No." Damon's eyes were as bleak as the Yorkshire moors in winter. "My God, what a romantic match we have made!"

He turned on his heel, stalked from the drawing room, and slammed out the door.

Chapter 16

After Damon's angry departure, Arabella fled upstairs to her room, followed by Beth.

"Arabella, you do not want to marry him," Beth cried. "You are doing it to save me from Mr. Dobbs."

"You are wrong. I do want to marry Damon. It is he who does not want to marry me," Arabella said grimly, then added in a happier voice, "I have wonderful news for you. Damon is giving you a small estate so that you and Justin can be married."

Beth's face glowed with sudden hope that slowly faded into doubt. "But why would he do that? He doesn't know either Justin or me. You asked him, didn't you, Arabella? That is why you said you would marry a man you have known less than a hour."

"I did not ask him," Arabella said wearily. "He offered. Furthermore, I have known Damon far longer than an hour, and I love him!"

Beth stared dumbfounded at Arabella. Swearing Beth to secrecy, Arabella told her the story of her meeting with Damon, leaving Beth torn between gratitude and horror at what her sister had done for her.

As Beth started to leave, she said reluctantly, "There is

something I must tell you about Damon. He . . . he . . . is the man that was with Sally Cromwell yesterday. The man Lady Vaughn says is her lover.''

Arabella's heart felt as though it were crumbling into dust. She remembered how staunchly Sally had defended Damon at Squire Mobley's dinner. Was that why?

When Brom returned home that night, he came straight to Arabella's room, still in his dusty and stained riding breeches.

He demanded without preamble, ''Will I like your betrothed?''

Arabella, amused by her brother's priorities, replied, ''I think so. He is your Mr. Smith.''

Brom's face glowed with excitement. ''Did he tell you?''

''He did not have to. You see, I am the friend who told him about you.''

''You knew him! And you didn't tell me!'' Brom's eyes were full of reproach. ''You knew how desperately I wanted to find out who he was.''

''Not nearly as much as I wanted you to. I knew no more about him than you did, not even his name. Although in retrospect I think I must have been peabrained not to have guessed who he was.''

''How did you meet him?'' Brom demanded.

Arabella swore him to secrecy as she had Beth and then told him the story. Brom was jubilant.

''Those dead highwaymen were the talk of London, especially when no one came forth to collect the reward,'' he exclaimed. ''By Jove, I can't think of anyone I would rather have you marry!''

Lady Vaughn did not arise from her bed the following morning. Instead she summoned her bosom-bow, Mrs. Berrey, to her side and treated her to a highly original version of Arabella's betrothal.

"I cannot tell you how sick I am about it," Lady Vaughn wailed as she delicately applied an embroidered handkerchief of white linen to her eyes to dry nonexistent tears. "I am so overset that I am quite unable to leave my bed. Arabella, willful chit that she is, insists upon marrying him—I am sure merely to embarrass us all and especially to disoblige me, for she knows how particularly I detest Damon Howard. She knows how utterly ineligible he is, but Arabella has always delighted in the most shocking behavior. What a trial she has been to me."

Lady Vaughn gave a lugubrious sigh befitting a patient and long-suffering saint. "I have done my best, but I declare she is the most contrary, mulish girl alive. Nothing will persuade her of Howard's ineligibility. I urged my husband to prohibit the match. But he would not dream of denying that chit anything she desired and has given his reluctant consent over my objections. But I have told him that they will not be married from Lindley Hall or in my presence. So they say they will be wed in London instead. I am surprised they don't elope to Gretna Green."

"But how did they meet?" Mrs. Berrey asked when at last she could manage to squeeze in a question.

The question momentarily disconcerted Her Ladyship, but she recovered quickly. "No doubt on one of her wild rides about the countryside. I have repeatedly begged my husband to curb her hoydenish ways, but he is so proud of her horsemanship he will not hear of it." Her Ladyship hastily sought to cut off any further embarrassing questions from her friend. "Oh, my dear Mrs. Berrey, I must beg you to leave me rest now. I fear I am about to have another spasm."

Lady Vaughn again dabbed at her eyes with her embroidered handkerchief and watched Mrs. Berrey's departure with satisfaction, knowing that her bosom-bow, who loved nothing so much as spreading gossip, would by nightfall have broadcast Her Ladyship's version of the betrothal throughout the countryside.

Mrs. Berrey exceeded Lady Vaughn's most optimistic expectations. By early afternoon it seemed everyone within fifty miles knew of Arabella's betrothal. A stream of shocked callers descended upon Lindley Park. Lady Vaughn declined to see them with the excuse that she was ill abed from shock and dismay at her stepdaughter's disgraceful betrothal.

So Arabella was left to deal with the callers. Lady Vaughn had unwittingly made this task easier by the tale she had told Mrs. Berrey. Arabella was very popular in the neighborhood, and most of the visitors came out of concern for her happiness. But she assured them with quiet dignity that she loved Damon and wished to marry him. That much, at least, was true. When she was asked how she had met him, she replied that he had chanced upon her after she had taken a fall from a horse while out riding and that, for her at least, it had been love at first sight.

By midafternoon, Lady Vaughn was so alarmed by the number of callers that she ordered Arabella to stop receiving them. Arabella was happy to oblige her stepmother, for she wished to write Aunt Margaret to plead for her cooperation.

It was a letter that Arabella never finished, for shortly after she began it, the duchess's post chaise pulled up at Lindley Hall.

Her arrival was enough to propel Lady Vaughn, in a ruffled satin dressing gown, from her bedchamber to greet the unexpected visitor. Her Ladyship was certain that the duchess would be an ally in her efforts to spike Arabella's betrothal.

Seeing the cold angry set of Her Grace's face, Lady Vaughn instantly regretted having quit her bed. She began a hurried synopsis of the tale that she had told Mrs. Berrey.

But she was brought up short by the duchess. "Balderdash! Save your taradiddles for more gullible creatures than

I.'' The duchess swept Lady Vaughn with a look of such exquisite disgust that Her Ladyship very nearly suffered a real spasm. ''Arabella is marrying Damon Howard to save her father from being thrown into prison for the debts incurred by your outrageous extravagances.''

Arabella led her aunt into the small sitting room off the drawing room, where the duchess took the precaution of locking the door against interruption. She turned to her niece and asked abruptly, ''Where did you meet Damon Howard?''

''He was introduced to me last evening—''

''I asked where you met him, not when you were introduced to him,'' the duchess said bluntly. ''Do not play the same sort of word games with me that he did!''

''You have been to see Damon?'' Arabella cried.

''Yes. I was persuaded that I would get a more honest accounting of your betrothal from him than ever I would from your father or stepmother. He was most candid about your father's visit to Willow Wood and, indeed, about everything but how and where you had met each other.''

''What made you think he knew me before we were introduced last night?'' Arabella parried.

''Because he is far too sensible a man to marry a woman he did not know. He was so very careful not to betray how he met you that I know I shall not like it.''

''He did not betray it because he promised me that he would not tell, and he is a man of his word,'' Arabella said. ''But you are right. You will not like the story.''

The duchess, after hearing it, readily agreed. Then she asked abruptly, ''How do you feel about marrying Damon?''

Arabella's confusion was mirrored in her face.

''You do not like him?'' the duchess asked quickly.

''To the contrary, I love him.''

''Then why such a face?''

"I am so ashamed. Papa offered to sell me to Damon. He—"

"All that matters, my dear child," the duchess said firmly, "is that you love him."

Before Arabella could protest that what mattered was that Damon did not love her, her aunt said, "You shall be married from my house in London, and I shall endeavor in the meager time we have to make it the most elaborate wedding of the season."

Arabella clapped her hands in delight and hugged her aunt. Such a wedding would virtually assure Damon of the ton's acceptance. "Oh, Aunt Margaret, you are so good to me."

"You will come back to London with me now. We have not much time, and we can draw up the wedding plans as we travel. Hurry upstairs and pack a portmanteau."

Arabella was only too happy to escape Lindley Park, but she wanted to see Damon first. She did not want to leave without having explained to him that she had never loved Estes. She said timidly, "Must we go so quickly? Could we not wait until morning?"

"No," the duchess said impatiently. "We will leave now. By the way, I understand that Damon is giving Beth a small estate so that she can marry Justin Keats. How did you manage to wheedle that out of Damon?"

"I did not even ask him. He offered it."

"He is very generous to you."

Yes, Arabella thought sadly, very generous with everything but his love.

Chapter 17

Arabella, with fear in her heart and a false smile on her lips, walked on quaking limbs up the aisle of Saint George's Church in Hanover Square in London. She leaned on her father's arm. The weighty splendor of her wedding gown, with its long train of satin edged with pearls and lace, was like an anchor dragging at her as she moved slowly, reluctantly up the long aisle toward the tall, dark figure that awaited her at the altar.

Through the layers of her veil, she saw that the church was crowded with the London ton. Damon should be well pleased.

As she neared the altar, her gaze traveled beyond the filled pews to where her bridegroom stood. Her heart seemed to somersault. How handsome he looked, so cool and composed. It was the first time that she had seen Damon since he had stalked out of Lindley Park after learning that she had previously been betrothed to Lord Estes.

Damon had planned to arrive in London a week before the wedding, but he had not come. Instead, he wrote Arabella that his father had taken a turn for the worse and was now too ill to travel to London to the wedding he had so wanted for his son. Damon's disappointment that his father could not attend the wedding was evident in his letter. Because of concern for his father, Damon wrote that he would not come up to London until the day of the wedding. He wished also to forgo a wedding trip and return immediately to Willow Wood.

As Arabella had refolded this brief, hastily written, and strangely impersonal note from the man who would soon be her husband, tears had glistened in her eyes.

Now, her long slow march down the aisle of Saint George's seemed to Arabella to be simultaneously the longest and the shortest walk of her life. She reached the altar, and her father placed her cold hand in Damon's warm one. She studied him through her veil. His face was an emotionless mask, his brown eyes cool and unreadable, his lips unsmiling.

His cold demeanor did nothing to quiet her fear as she stood before the altar with him. Everyone who had attended her before the ceremony had said what a beautiful bride she made in her white satin and lace gown. French lace and hundreds of tiny pearls decorated its carefully fitted bodice. A stand-up collar of lace encircled the high neck. The sleeves were puffs of satin over her upper arms that gave way to fitted lace reaching to her wrists. From her tiny waist cascaded yards and yards of satin and lace that culminated in the long train. It was a gown fit for a queen.

Yet Damon hardly seemed to notice it—or her.

It was only through sheer willpower that Arabella managed to speak her vows in a calm, strong voice that gave no hint of her inner fears. But when Damon attempted to put a gold-and-diamond wedding band on her finger, her hand shook so that he had great difficulty in sliding it onto her ring finger. She fixed her eyes on her quaking extremity and the dazzling ring to avoid the sharp, searching look that his dark eyes gave her.

The festivities following the wedding were held at the duchess of Hampshire's mansion in Berkeley Square. She rarely entertained, and an invitation from her was much prized. That coupled with curiosity over Damon Howard and his marriage to the duchess's niece assured that everyone who had been invited came, even though in some cases it meant returning to London from country estates a considerable distance away.

The guests were amply rewarded. Aunt Margaret had outdone herself for the wedding celebration. It would be the talk of London for weeks to come.

Arabella forced herself to look as though she were the happiest of brides. She gazed at her husband with the pride of a woman who might have just captured in wedlock a prince of royal blood. She was determined to still any speculation about the real reasons for their marriage.

But most of all she wanted to insure that the ton accepted Damon. The best way of doing this was to demonstrate that hers was a love match that had the full approval of all her prestigious relatives. At least, she thought bitterly, it was a love match on her part. If only Damon loved her in return, she would truly have been the happiest of brides.

It was easy for her to be proud of him. Once he had crossed her aunt's threshold, he had displayed the gracefulness and easy self-assurance of a born aristocrat. His conversation was intelligent and witty. His manners were charming.

Arabella overheard one stuffy dowager of impressive title say to another, "Who would ever have believed that this fine, well-bred gentleman could be that notorious Damon Howard? He is not at all what I expected. I, for one, am astounded."

Arabella overheard several similar remarks, indicating that the astounded dowager had considerable company among her fellow guests. It was clear that Damon now had what he so wanted: the ton's acceptance.

Arabella was far less sure, however, whether she had any place at all in his heart. Although he matched her in his public display of his regard for her, it was evident that he was playing a role. He talked easily to others, but in the rare moments that he was alone with Arabella, he was silent. Sometimes when they were separated, she would catch him looking at her. He would immediately look away, a peculiar expression on his tanned face.

When she did manage to engage his brown eyes, which could be so lively and teasing, they were like shuttered windows that gave not the slightest hint of what he was thinking.

Throughout the afternoon, Arabella heard only one ugly remark. She had slipped away to freshen up and was returning to the festivities in the ballroom when she happened upon the harpy nicknamed Lady Snipe and her companion. Neither woman saw Arabella.

"How sorry I feel for the poor bride," Lady Snipe said. "Only think she might have been a countess, but instead she has had to settle for a by-blow begotten on a serving slut."

Arabella was infuriated by this evil slander of Damon's mother, and she rounded on Lady Snipe. "Nell Fitzhugh was not a serving slut! She was one of the most beautiful, charming, accomplished women that it has ever been my privilege to know. And you need not pity me! I would rather be married to her son than to the king!"

Arabella turned and, still shaking with anger, stumbled blindly back into the hallway and a tall broad figure. Looking up, she saw her husband and realized with sinking heart that he, too, had heard Lady Snipe's evil remark. To her surprise, he did not seem angry, but strangely amused.

"That insufferable woman," Arabella complained.

His voice was cool, emotionless. "I suggest that in the future you ignore such remarks. If you attempt to defend me and my mother against all our detractors, you will be kept very busy."

"But—"

"I am quite used to such remarks. It has been a long time

since they have had the power to disturb me," Damon said calmly, putting her arm in his and leading her back into the ballroom.

"I am sorry that your father could not be here," Arabella said softly, touching his arm. "I know how much his presence would have meant to you and to him."

Damon's face reflected his sadness. Just then Brom bounded up. When he had arrived in London with Lord Vaughn and Beth three days before the wedding, Arabella had been startled by the change in him. The sullen rebellion and irritable boredom were gone. When she had asked her father about the change in her brother, he replied that he had not noticed. In fact, he had seen little of Brom since her departure for London. Her brother had been spending most of his time with Damon at Willow Wood.

Now Brom's thin, angular face was alive with an enthusiasm and excitement that Arabella had not seen there in months.

"Arabella," he cried, "can I come live with you at Willow Wood?"

She was dismayed because she was acutely conscious of how much Damon had already done for her family. She could not repay him by foisting her brother off on him.

"Oh, Brom," Arabella said lightly, "you would be so bored. You said London is the only spot for you."

"No more," he assured her. "Willow Wood is much more exciting. Damon has been showing me all sorts of fascinating things. He says I may live there if you and Father agree."

"You must ask Papa first," Arabella parried.

Brom rushed off in search of his father.

Arabella said to her husband, "You most likely will be stuck with him. Papa will be glad for the excuse to be rid of him."

"Do you object to his living with us?" Damon asked.

Arabella blinked at him in surprise. "Of course not. I shall be happy to have him away from Lady Vaughn. The two are disastrous together. But it is you I am thinking of." She looked up at him with shining eyes. "You have been so good to us already. I cannot ask you to take my brother, too."

He smiled. "You did not ask me. He did, and I want to."

"Arabella." Brom was back at his sister's side. "Papa gives his permission for me to live at Willow Wood."

By the time Arabella went to change from her wedding dress into a traveling gown for the return to Willow Wood, many of the guests had already departed. The afternoon had been a huge success.

As Arabella fastened the jet buttons that ran the length of her blue silk traveling gown, she could no longer push from her mind what lay ahead of her this night. She was beset by a lively dread of the moment when she must at last be alone with Damon. The fear her stepmother had instilled in her would not be vanquished, especially when Damon had seemed so cold and distant to her today.

When she finished with the buttons, she gave herself a final appraisal in the mirror. More jets set in concentric half circles decorated the gown's top like strands of black pearls. On her head she wore a matching hat with a wide brim and sweeping feather.

She went down the stairs to rejoin her husband and her aunt, who were waiting for her in the hall below after having bidden farewell to a group of departing guests.

Suddenly the front door was flung violently open and Lord Estes stalked in.

Arabella, who was on the final step, nearly tripped and fell at the sight of him. Damon caught her and held her close to steady her. His nearness and the strength of his grasp so thrilled her that it nearly overpowered her apprehension at seeing Lord Estes.

How different he looked now from the man she had known. His stylish clothes had been tossed carelessly on. Their wrinkled condition proclaimed that they had been treated equally carelessly when he was not wearing them. His blond hair, which used to be so precisely curled, hung in oily clumps. His lower face sported a ragged blond stubble. His slate-blue eyes were bloodshot.

He staggered as he crossed the threshold, and Arabella realized that he was drunk.

The duchess, sizing Estes up at a glance, hurried him into a small unused sitting room. He allowed her to do so but called loudly over his shoulder to Damon, "I want to talk to you, bastard."

Arabella shuddered and looked around quickly. The hall was empty, and none of the few remaining guests seemed to have heard the commotion.

Damon's eyes reflected his loathing of his half brother, but his voice was polite. "Of course, although I deplore the timing and location of your request."

Damon followed Estes into the sitting room. Arabella hurried in after him and shut the heavy door firmly behind her.

"You are foxed," Damon said to Estes. "Drink, not gambling, is the devil that is destroying you. It addles your brain and makes you mean."

Estes seemed not to hear him. Instead he snarled, "So you were not satisfied with stealing my fortune from me; you had to steal my betrothed as well, bastard."

"You are in error on two counts," Damon said calmly. "First, I did not steal your betrothed, because you had already broken it off. Second, I believe there is considerable question as to which of us is the bastard."

Estes reeled back in shock, and he gasped. "So now you mean to try to rob me of my title, too!"

"You are welcome to the title. I have no desire for it, and I will not challenge the legitimacy of your claim to it."

Arabella wondered why a man who had just married to at-tain social position would now disclaim any interest in an earldom.

Estes sneered. "So you are content with merely stealing one of the largest fortunes in England from me. I have a mind to call you out."

"Really?" Damon said in a voice heavy with incredulity. "Face-to-face? But that is not at all in your style."

"You cur!" Estes sputtered.

Damon's eyes were like cold steel. "If you wish to call me out, I shall be only too happy to accommodate you. Issue your challenge."

"This is madness," the duchess interjected. "Estes is no match for you with any weapon, Damon."

The duchess's words reminded Estes of his half brother's legendary dueling skills, which, in His Lordship's drunken state, he had forgotten. He sobered instantly and then paled with fear. "No, no, I won't. I see what you are up to, bastard. You are trying to trick me into calling you out so that you may kill me before I produce an heir. Then my title will be yours."

Arabella watched Estes with as much loathing as Damon. She directed a silent prayer of thanks heavenward that she had escaped being married to such a weak, disgusting creature.

Damon told Estes patiently, "You were the one that broached the subject of a duel, not I. And I have told you that I have no interest in your title."

"Only in my fortune." Estes's eyes blazed with hatred. "You turned my father against me. You got him to cut me off and give you everything."

"You know that is not true," Damon said firmly. "It was you and only you who turned him against you. You know your unspeakable deed that did it. You know, too, that you have no one to blame but yourself."

The look on Estes's face was horrible to behold. He gave a smothered sob and rushed to the sitting room door. As he flung it open, he stormed back at Damon. "I wish you happy—married to a woman who adores me."

Estes ran down the hall and out the door.

Damon looked coldly at Arabella. "Perhaps you would prefer to go with your adored."

She stared at her husband, too aghast to answer.

As he turned away from her, she saw the bitter hurt in his eyes. "If not, we shall leave immediately for Willow Wood."

Chapter 18

Arabella and Damon left Berkeley Square for Willow Wood in his well-sprung post chaise drawn by a magnificent double pair of grays.

Although Damon had been so calm during his confrontation with his half brother, it had left him brooding and silent. Since the door of the post chaise had closed upon them, he had said nothing. Indeed, he had scarcely even glanced at his bride. Instead, he had stared out the window, lost in bitter thought. Damon was not quite so close to Arabella on the green velvet cushions that their bodies touched but close enough to disquiet her heart and mind.

His brooding silence began to weigh heavily on Arabella's already overburdened nerves. She stared out the window without interest at the jostling crowds that shared the street with the post chaise. If only she knew how to break through the wall that Damon had erected between them.

Faced with her husband's dark and forbidding countenance, she dreaded mentioning Estes's name. Still she ached to assure Damon that Estes's claim that she adored him was totally false.

Chastising herself for being such a pudding heart, Arabella asked hesitantly, "What unspeakable thing did Lord Estes do that turned your father against him?"

Damon turned to her, scowling. "I told you never to mention Estes's name to me."

"Why do you hate him so?"

Damon glared at her. "I will not discuss him."

His brusque unreasonableness fired her own temper. "As you wish!" She closed her eyes and leaned her head back against the velvet squabs.

But she found no peace from her churning emotions. Damon's coldness heightened the fear instilled in her by Lady Vaughn. There seemed to be no tenderness or love at all in him, only barely repressed anger. Darkness was already settling about the post chaise, and with each passing mile, Arabella's dread of what lay ahead of her grew.

After the equipage left London behind, its pace quickened until it was traveling at an alarming speed. When it hit a series of potholes, its occupants were bounced about viciously. Damon braced himself and automatically reached out to draw Arabella against him so that she would not be tossed about.

"Must we go so fast?" Arabella exclaimed, unnerved by the warmth and pleasant masculine scent of her husband.

"Traveling leisurely across the countryside in a post chaise is not the way I desire to spend my wedding night," Damon replied.

In the pale light cast by the coach's two gilded bronze lanterns, Damon's eyes perused her in such a coolly possessive and intimate fashion that she had no doubt as to what his desire was. She shivered under his scrutiny.

Seeing her uneasiness, Damon said sarcastically, "Such eagerness to sample the delights of marriage. Remember our bargain."

"I have given you no reason to complain."

"Not yet," he said coldly.

"Nor will I," she cried hotly, determined to endure whatever he desired without complaint. Her face mirrored her un-happy thoughts.

Seeing it, Damon withdrew his protective arm from about her. "Damn it, Arabella, I wanted no unwilling wife. I told you not to marry me unless you were willing to give yourself to me fully."

"And I mean to! You cannot fault me. I have done every-thing that you asked of me."

"Yes," he said scornfully. "I must congratulate you on the fine performance that you gave today. Had I not known better, I would have thought you were delighted by your mar-riage and very much in love with your husband. How much that must have cost your pride."

She was both shocked and stung by his cold dismissal of her efforts. In truth, they had cost her pride nothing. But now, in the face of his scorn, that pride would not let her admit to a man who cared naught for her that she loved him. Instead, she cried angrily, "You got what you wanted today: the so-cial acceptance that you so desperately desire."

His eyes mocked her. "I have other desires that I expect to be satisfied tonight."

How cold and uncaring he was. Arabella bowed her head and turned away from him so that he might not see the fear in her eyes at the thought of what she could expect at his hands tonight.

But even in the dim lantern light of the carriage, Damon's sharp eyes missed nothing. "How unhappy you look. Is it because you are afraid that our neighbors at Willow Wood will ostracize you?" His question was cool, almost de-tached.

"Of course not," she cried indignantly. "If they are so poor-hearted that they cannot bring themselves to accept me *and* my husband, I have no wish for their friendship."

Damon studied her, obviously perplexed.

They rode on through the night in silence until they turned off the road onto the lane that led to Willow Wood.

"Why did you and your father return to Willow Wood now after having left it shut for so many years?" Arabella asked.

"For years my father could not bear to go there because it reminded him too much of my mother and her loss. He adored her." The pain in Damon's eyes told Arabella how much he, too, had adored his mother. "But when my father was dying, he suddenly wanted to go back, I think because Mama is buried at Willow Wood in a little glade that she loved, and he felt closer to her. He so wanted to return that when he rallied and improved enough to travel, I brought him back."

"Will you—we—stay at Willow Wood long?"

"It is up to my father," Damon replied. "I much prefer Longbridge, the estate in Sussex where we have made our home for the past decade. I would like to give you full freedom to make what changes you want to Willow Wood. But my father wishes it to remain much as it was when my mother was alive."

"I shall not mind that," Arabella assured him, recalling how as a tiny child she had loved her visits to Nell's charming little house. "I loved it when I was little."

When the post chaise stopped at Willow Wood, pale moonlight illuminated its two-story brick house with a white pillared portico. It was not large as country houses went, but it was handsome.

As Damon helped Arabella down from the equipage, the door of the house opened. An elderly, wizened servant stepped out upon the portico and bowed to them.

Damon introduced Turpin, the butler, to Arabella, then asked him with worried eyes and concerned voice, "How is my father?"

"He has been very restless and uneasy since you left, but he is no worse."

A shadow passed over Damon's face. "I will go to him at once."

"May I go with you?" Arabella asked.

"The earl is asleep," Turpin said.

"We won't disturb him," Damon said.

As he led Arabella up the stairs, she recalled all the speculation that she had heard in London about the earl's mysterious illness. "What does your father suffer from?"

A frown creased Damon's strong face. "I am sorry, Arabella, but I cannot tell you. He has forbidden me to discuss it."

She blinked in astonishment. "Why? Is it contagious?"

"No," he said angrily. "Nor is it a social disease. But I am bound by my promise to him."

"What is a social disease?" Arabella asked innocently.

Her question clearly startled Damon. For the first time since they had left London, a smile danced on his lips. "That is not at all the thing I want to explain to my bride on our wedding day," he replied wryly.

He stopped in front of a door at the back of the house. As he put his hand on the doorknob, he told Arabella, "Wait by the door for me."

She followed him inside and did as he bade. He approached the tester bed near the windows. A single candle flickered on a bedside table, illuminating a male attendant who sat patiently in a chair beside the bed. Arabella could not make out the figure beneath the covers, but the sound of his painful, labored breathing filled the room.

Damon stood beside the bed, looking down at his sleeping father for several minutes with such love that Arabella was deeply moved. If only Damon could feel so much love for his wife.

As Damon escorted her from the room, she saw the pain in his eyes. Instinctively, she reached out and touched his arm to try to comfort him. "I know how hard it is to watch someone you love suffer."

Damon nodded at her bleakly, but there was gratitude in his eyes for her understanding.

He led her into a large room adjacent to his father's apartment that clearly belonged to a man. There were no feminine frills or delicately carved furniture in it. From the sturdy posters of the great tester bed to the large armchairs, the furnishings were all substantial. The bed hangings and the window draperies were of heavy burgundy velvet. An interior door connected the room to the earl's.

To her surprise she saw that her own baggage had been neatly stacked in one corner. "Where is my room?" she asked uneasily.

"Here."

"But surely this is yours," she said faintly.

"Ours now." He grinned at her. "Don't look so discomforted. Blame it on my low birth that I do not hold with silly aristocratic notions of separate bedchambers for husband and wife."

He reached up and, with a deftness that betrayed much experience, unpinned her plumed hat, removed it from her head, and tossed it upon an oak chest.

"Let me help you," Damon said, beginning to unfasten the topmost black jet button at the neck of her gown.

Arabella instinctively drew back at his touch. A deeply rosy blush spread over her face. "I will summon a maid to help me," she stammered in embarrassment.

"Don't be silly." His fingers had rapidly disposed of the first few buttons. "I will attend to you."

Arabella pulled away from him, her modesty affronted. "But, but you cannot watch me undress."

"Nonsense. I am your husband. I told you that I would insist upon all of my marital rights. Now let me help you." His fingers returned to their prey.

Arabella stiffened. Then remembering her duty, she closed her eyes, gritted her teeth, and, holding herself rigid, forced herself to let him proceed.

His fingers fell away from the buttons and took her hand. "Are you afraid of me, Arabella?" His voice was troubled.

"No. Yes. I don't know," she blurted, keeping her eyes tightly closed. She was trembling now.

Gently he put his hands on her arms and guided her to the bed. She sank down on it, grateful for its support.

He smoothed her hair with gentle fingers. "What have I done to you to make you so afraid of me?" he asked softly.

To her surprise she could offer no coherent answer to his question. Finally she faltered, "It is not what you have done but what you want of me."

His voice, very near her ear, was low and soft. "I do not think, Arabella, that wishing to make love to you qualifies me as a beast."

"It is different for a man. For a woman, it is what she must endure." Arabella unconsciously repeated Lady Vaughn's inflections as well as some of her words.

Sudden comprehension flared in Damon's eyes. "Did your stepmother tell you what to expect tonight?"

Arabella nodded, her face flaming. "I am afraid I was very ignorant. I had little notion of what . . ." Her voice faded away.

"Lady Vaughn frightened you a great deal, didn't she?"

Arabella confessed, "It was what drove me to write that terrible letter to you."

Damon swore softly. Then he cupped her frightened face in his hand. His head lowered and his lips touched her mouth with a kiss so sweet and gentle that Arabella felt as though she had just tasted the nectar of nature's sweetest flower.

When he lifted his lips from hers, he asked, "Dear Arabella, have you ever known Lady Vaughn to be right about anything before?"

She looked at him in surprise. "No—o—o."

He stroked her face gently. The shuttered look was gone from his velvet-brown eyes, replaced by a tenderness that warmed her like a glowing fire. "Nor is she this time."

Arabella stared at him, suspended between hope and fear.

His hands gently unfastened the pins in her hair, loosening it about her shoulders. "Let me demonstrate to you how wrong your stepmother is."

And so he did with infinite patience, beginning with a soft rain of tender kisses upon her brow, her cheek, the tip of her upturned nose. His lips did not claim her mouth but moved down to the curve of her throat. His hands stole to her hair and gently removed its restraining pins so that it tumbled down about her shoulders in luxurious waves.

His mouth laid a trail of kisses along her neck as it moved to her lips. His hands stroked her hair and her cheeks. Slowly, so very slowly, he increased the tempo of his assault upon her senses and her desire. When his fingers returned to the buttons of her gown, she trembled again, but this time in excitement, not fear. Her body yearned for him, for his touch, as it had never hungered for anything before. he was kindling a fire in her that flamed higher and higher, stoked by his slow, intimate caresses, until it consumed them both.

Finally when, breathless with wonder and rapture, she fell asleep in her husband's arms, she felt so safe, so contented, so happy. How nice it would be, she thought dreamily as sleep claimed her, to open her eyes on the morrow and come slowly awake in his arms.

But it was not to be.

Arabella did not awaken until midmorning. In that first moment when she was still more asleep than awake, she was suffused with warm, dreamy memories of the night's pleasures. How afraid she had been. She should have known that Damon could not be the beast that her stepmother had painted him.

Lady Vaughn had been right in only one respect. Arabella's introduction to love was indeed beyond imagining. But it was an experience of beauty, thanks to Damon's patience and skill, not of agony. There was one brief moment of pain. He warned her it would happen—but only briefly and only once. Then he made her forget it in the explosion of pleasure that soon followed.

Now, as she came awake, Arabella, warmed by the glow of her love for Damon, wanted only to feel his arms about her again and to tell him how wonderful he was.

Sleepily she reached out to caress him, but her hand encountered only emptiness. Her eyes flew open, and she saw that he had quit the room as well as the bed. Beset by disappointment, she got up and dressed. The bed without Damon seemed strangely alien and uninviting to her.

His absence shook her to the core. Did he care so little for her that he could not even remain this first morning with her until she awakened?

Arabella was finishing coiling her long thick chestnut hair, when a knock sounded on the door and a large-boned, gray-haired woman with a no-nonsense air about her entered.

She told Arabella, "I am Mrs. Purdie, the housekeeper. Your husband asked me to give you a tour of the house if you would like it."

The offer stung Arabella. She wanted Damon and no one else to show her her new home. But she had nothing else to do. Feeling unloved and neglected by her husband, she reluctantly accepted the housekeeper's offer.

The house was little changed from the way Arabella remembered it. Aunt Nell had favored elegant French furnishings and floral-chintz upholstery and drapes. Her taste as well as her fine collection of porcelain was much in evidence about the house. Although it was small for a country house, it had been cleverly decorated by Nell to give it an inviting air of cheerful comfort.

Arabella and Mrs. Purdie were in a sunny workroom at the back of the house where flowers were arranged when Damon's voice was heard in the entry hall. Arabella, who had been examining the vases and bowls that lined the shelves of the workroom, hurried out, but she found only a maid dusting in the hall.

"Where is Mr. Howard?" Arabella asked.

The maid curtsied. "Went up to see his father, ma'am."

Arabella was deeply hurt. Instead of seeking out his bride of a day, Damon had gone directly to his father. She took this as another indication of how little affection Damon held for her.

This realization made her awkward and ill-at-ease when fifteen minutes later Damon found her sitting in a wing chair in the drawing room.

"I did not expect to see you up yet," he said cheerfully as he entered. "You were sleeping so soundly that I thought surely you would continue to do so until noon. I had to get up because I have so much to catch up on." A note of concern sounded in his voice. "I hope I didn't waken you when I left."

"No," Arabella said stiffly. She did not rise to go to him but remained seated. She could think of nothing to say, and she avoided his eyes, afraid of the unsettling effect they had on her. Instead she stared down at her hands folded in her lap.

She could feel his puzzled gaze upon her as he crossed to her chair. Still she did not look up at him.

"Did Mrs. Purdie show you around?"

Damon's question revived the hurt that Arabella had felt when she had learned that he had delegated this to the housekeeper. She swallowed hard and nodded, still not looking at him.

"What the devil's the matter, Arabella?" he demanded with sudden fierceness.

What could she tell him: that she wanted his love? He would only point out to her that his love had not been part of the bargain he had made with her father and her.

"Nothing," she gulped.

His hands, which the night before had been so gentle and exciting, seized her arms roughly and lifted her out of the chair to her feet. "Look at me, Arabella! I want to know what is bothering you."

Trapped in his painful grip, she stared silently up at his aristocratic face, with its broad forehead beneath the thick black hair and hard, jutting chin. His eyes were as fierce as his grip. She loved him so. Her heart ached at the sight and touch of him.

"Nothing," she lied, but she knew that her eyes betrayed her. "You are hurting my arms."

With a muttered oath, he released her and said wearily, "My father wants to see you. I'll take you up to him."

When they reached the top of the steps, Damon stopped suddenly, turned to Arabella, his face sterner than she had ever seen it, and said, "Under no circumstances are you ever to mention Estes in my father's presence. He cannot bear to hear his name."

Arabella wondered again what unspeakable thing Estes had done to earn his father's hatred.

Chapter 19

Although Arabella knew that the earl of Woodthorpe had been at death's door, she was still shocked when she approached his bedside. At her mother's funeral, he had been a man of fifty and possessing robust vitality. He had been almost as tall and broad as Damon, with thick black hair only lightly seasoned with gray. Now, looking down at the frail, shrunken figure in the big tester bed, she could scarcely believe he was the same man. His hair was thin and white; his face was that of an old man who had suffered much.

She hid her shock behind a bright smile.

"How like your mother you look when you smile," the earl said. He turned to his son. "I know you have a great many things to attend to, Damon. Why don't you go, and your wife and I will get acquainted."

Damon looked relieved. "I do have so much to do," he told Arabella. "With father so ill, I neglected things sadly in recent weeks, and I am also instituting some agricultural changes at our estates here in Kent that I must oversee."

After Damon left, the earl's hollow, suffering eyes were immensely sad. "How I wanted to be at your wedding. Tell me about it."

Arabella complied in great detail, hoping to erase some of

the earl's sadness with the fullness of her account. Knowing how much he wanted his son accepted by society, she was careful to list all the illustrious members of the ton that had attended and to tell him the many remarks that she had overheard indicating how impressed they had been with Damon. Her account obviously delighted him.

Arabella spent the rest of the morning with the earl, entertaining him with amusing stories about London and her life at Lindley Park.

After they had lunch together, the earl fell asleep. He was still napping when Sally Cromwell came to call. She looked especially lovely in an emerald-green riding outfit that matched her eyes and enhanced her pale skin.

"It was such a lovely day for a ride that I came on horseback," she explained to Arabella.

As Arabella led her friend into the drawing room, Sally queried in disappointment, "Isn't Damon here?"

Surprised, Arabella asked, "Did you come to see him?"

"I came to see you both. No one can talk of anything but your marriage."

"Will I be an outcast?" Arabella asked, realizing that she did not care.

"No, not at all," Sally assured her. "Everyone is eager to call on you, and they will accept Damon for your sake. You have nothing to fear."

Arabella was more relieved for Damon than for herself. At least their marriage was bringing Damon what he most wanted.

"How unjust people here have been to Damon," Sally said. "It was not at all like that in Sussex when he lived at Longbridge. He was accepted by everyone."

No wonder Damon preferred Longbridge, Arabella thought.

Sally continued. "Even the servants and tenants at Longbridge loved him. He was always so concerned about their welfare.''

Arabella said nothing. *Just as he was concerned about a wife he didn't want.*

Sally smiled. ''Now tell me about your wedding.''

When Arabella finished her account, Sally asked with a knowing smile, ''And what do you think of your husband now?''

Arabella was startled. ''What do you mean?''

''Damon has a reputation of being a consummate lover. He cut quite a swath among the ladies in Sussex, who found him irresistible in bed.''

Sally said this with the easy frankness that had always before endeared her to Arabella, but the effect was very different this time. Pain stabbed at Arabella's heart, and she wondered wildly, *As irresistible as I found him last night?*

Jealousy gripped Arabella. She remembered again what Lady Vaughn had said about a man not caring with whom he satisfied his lusts so long as they were satisfied. No wonder Damon had not bothered to wait for her to awaken this morning. She might be his wife, but she was also just one of the many women who had shared his bed.

Suddenly Arabella straightened as though she had been stabbed with a sharp shard of glass. Lady Vaughn had been so certain that Sally and Damon were lovers. Arabella stared with frozen anguish at her friend. Were they? Had Sally been one of those Sussex ladies who found Damon irresistible?

Arabella was so distraught at the possibility that she could not force herself to ask the question aloud, but she was so numbed by it that she could think of nothing else to say either.

Sally, clearly puzzled by the abrupt change in Arabella, tried without much success to make conversation for a few more minutes, then quickly took her leave.

After she was gone, Arabella sat staring down at the gold-and-diamond band that Damon had placed upon her finger the previous day. If only he had given her his love with his ring. How painful it was to be wildly in love with a man who had reluctantly been persuaded to marry her. *"For social position, of course,"* he had said so offhandedly that day at Lindley Park.

Arabella went back up to the earl's room. But he was still asleep. She walked softly to the windows that overlooked the back of the house and offered a commanding view of the meadows and woods beyond the gardens of Willow Wood.

A spyglass lay on a low table by the windows. Arabella picked up the long cylinder and stared through it. From this vantage point she could see for a great distance. She could even make out the pretty little glade near a creek shaded by willows, that had been Nell's favorite spot. Arabella had spent pleasant hours there playing while her mama and Nell had talked.

Arabella moved the glass so that she could see nearer to the house. To her surprise, Damon's big bay and another horse, a frisky mare, were waiting by a large beech. She moved the glass slightly and saw that the two riders had dismounted and were standing together talking. Arabella focused the spyglass on the faces of the pair, then stifled a cry of dismay as she recognized Sally Cromwell with Damon.

Instead of riding homeward when she had left Arabella, Sally obviously had gone in the opposite direction in search of Damon. Now Sally was talking with animated excitement to him. Suddenly a delighted smile broke over Damon's face, and he seemed as excited and happy as Sally. Stunned, Arabella gripped the window edge for support and closed her eyes.

When Arabella opened them a moment later, Damon was helping Sally to mount. As she rode away, she turned with a bright smile on her lips and waved at him. He waved happily back. The sight was indelibly imprinted in Arabella's mind. Their faces convinced Arabella that Lady Vaughn was right.

Damon was Sally's lover. Arabella's eyes burned with tears of misery and jealousy.

She longed to race impetuously out of the house and confront Damon, but he would only remind her of her fatal letter inviting him to take a mistress. For the millionth time she cursed herself for having written it. Her desire in doing so had been to spare herself Damon's attentions. Now she no more wanted to do that than she wanted him to have a mistress.

Just then the earl awoke. Arabella wiped hastily at her eyes before turning to him. It took all the determination that she possessed to maintain a lighthearted, cheerful facade for the sick man.

Replacing the spyglass on the table, she asked him about it.

"I use it to look at Nell's grave," he said quietly. "We buried her in her favorite spot."

"The glade of willows by the creek?"

"You know it?"

"I used to go there with her and Mama."

Fearing that the earl would find speaking of Nell too distressing, Arabella began to regale him again with anecdotes about London and Lindley Park.

She and the earl were still talking amicably when Damon came in just before dinner. He was clearly delighted by the easy rapport between his wife and his father.

"If you don't mind," he said to Arabella, "I will have dinner brought up to us here so that we may have it with my father."

Arabella agreed. She felt less awkward with her husband when they were in her father-in-law's company.

She was haunted by the scene she had witnessed that afternoon between Damon and Sally. Finally she could stand it no longer and said, "Sally Cromwell called on me this afternoon."

"I know. I saw her, too," Damon said casually. "It must have eased your mind to know that you will not be ostracized by our neighbors."

Arabella bit her lip to keep from retorting that it was not her neighbors but her husband that she cared about.

After dinner, Damon and Arabella stayed with the earl until he showed signs of tiring. Arabella, who had known only an indifferent father, was amazed and warmed by the strong bond of love, respect, and companionship between the earl and Damon. It moved her deeply to watch them together and to listen to the easy camaraderie of their talk. Arabella had never seen a father and son so close. Their relationship was so unlike that of her own father and brother. How different Brom might be now if he had enjoyed the love and attention from Papa that Damon had clearly had from his father.

When at last Damon bade his father good night and guided Arabella through the connecting door to their own room, he closed the door swiftly behind them, wrapped her in his arms, and without a word, kissed her.

She stiffened in surprise at his unexpected move, but then the seductive power of his lips coaxed an answering response from her own. Her jealousy and unhappiness were forgotten in the enormous pleasure that his lips and his hands gave her as they roamed caressingly over her. She was helpless in his hands, and she made no protest as he carried her to the bed. No longer constricted by her fear that he would become a rutting monster such as Lady Vaughn had described, she found his lovemaking even more thrilling than the night before.

Long after Damon had fallen asleep, Arabella lay awake listening to his deep rhythmic breathing. How much she loved him and how painful to know that her love was not reciprocated.

Damon turned in his sleep and snuggled against her. His hand unconsciously caressed her hip. Still deeply asleep, he murmured, "My sweet, dearest love."

Arabella's heart froze. Whom had Damon mistaken her for in his sleep? Sally? Another woman from Sussex? Or an impatient London lady? A lump welled up in Arabella's throat. Whom did Damon love? Certainly not his wife, whom he had strongly objected to marrying at all. The word love had not crossed his lips when he was awake, not even at the ardent height of his passion this night or the previous.

Chapter 20

Brom came to stay at Willow Wood the next day, and life quickly settled into a pattern. Damon spent his days either closeted in his study, working on a seemingly endless stream of financial papers and accounts, or out on his estates, overseeing changes and improvements he had ordered. Wherever Damon went, Brom followed him like a puppy who would not let his master out of his sight.

Arabella marveled at the change that her husband wrought in Brom. Damon's patience, tact, and humor extinguished her brother's surliness and rebellion like water on fire. Damon's good-humored teasing mixed with cheerful understanding had succeeded where all of Lady Vaughn's harangues and her husband's rigid commands had failed.

Arabella saw almost nothing of Damon during the daytime. She was kept busy with visitors and the earl. Sally Cromwell had been right in her assessment of the countryside's reaction to Arabella's marriage. Everyone seemed eager to call upon her. When she was not receiving callers, she spent much of her time talking and reading to the earl, who made it clear how much he enjoyed her company.

In the evenings Arabella, Damon, his father, and Brom

dined together. After dinner, they talked or played cards. Occasionally Damon and his father played chess.

Damon was unfailingly polite and considerate to Arabella—and reserved. Whenever he looked at her, it was with shuttered, almost brooding eyes that enhanced the awkwardness she felt with him. Arabella's conviction grew that she was neglected and unloved by her husband.

Damon, Brom, and the earl all seemed satisfied with the emerging pattern of their lives at Willow Wood, but Arabella chafed for more privacy with her husband. The only time that they were alone together was after they had retired for the night, and that was not enough for her to explore the mysteries of this complex man and break down the invisible barrier that had grown up between them.

He remained as tender and thrilling a lover to her as he had been on their wedding night, but never once was there any mention of love between them. Arabella, for her part, was too mortified to tell a man who did not care for her how much she loved him.

The newlyweds received numerous invitations, but to Arabella's surprise, Damon seemed to have no enthusiasm for them.

"Pick only the ones you most want to accept," he told her with evident distaste, "and we will go."

She was perplexed that he was not eager to take advantage of the social acceptance that he had married to obtain, and she said, "But I thought you would want to accept them all."

He regarded her coldly. "Whatever made you think that?"

She turned away without answering. There was so much she did not know or understand about Damon. Arabella began to envy Brom for being on such easy terms with her husband.

Beth came to Willow Wood to visit. Justin Keats was expected home by the end of the month, and Beth could talk of nothing else. A choking lump formed in Arabella's throat.

How secure her sister was in her knowledge of Justin's love for her. Would Arabella ever be able to glory in the certainty of Damon's love as Beth did in Justin's?

The earl was improving rapidly now, and Arabella spent more and more time with him.

Ten days after her arrival at Willow Wood, Damon, clearly pleased, said, "The doctor is astonished at how rapidly my father has improved since you came. You have been wonderful medicine for him. I have not seen him so happy since Es—" Damon broke off abruptly, his eyes suddenly hard. "Since he got sick."

Before Arabella could ask Damon what he had started to say, he hastily changed the subject. "I am sorry that I have had so little time with you, but I am inundated with urgent matters that must be attended to. When my father was dying, I never left his bedside all those weeks, and now I am paying the price." He ran his fingers lightly along Arabella's cheek, and she marveled at how his touch thrilled her. "I hope you are not feeling too neglected."

It was exactly what she was feeling, but she did not confess it. Instead, she said, "I enjoy your father's company."

That much was true. She already knew more about the earl than she did about his son, who was her husband. Sometimes Woodthorpe told her anecdotes about her mama. Other times he talked about his enormous pride in Damon. He never mentioned Estes, however, and Arabella, mindful of her husband's warning, did not either.

One day when Arabella had picked a bouquet of Michaelmas daisies, bellflowers, and carnations to brighten the earl's bedside table, he said, "Nell loved flowers." He sighed and laid his head back against his pillows. "She was the only woman that I ever in my life loved. After she died, I tried to find another, but I never could. Nell was my true wife."

"Then why did you marry the countess?" Arabella blurted.

"To save Nell." He sighed and moved his frail head with its thin cap of white hair back. "I was still underage when she and I were married. My father dragged me back to Wood-thorpe Hall and lied to have the marriage annulled. He kept me a prisoner until I would agree to marry Henrietta. Mean-while, Nell was destitute and pregnant with Damon. She was alone, friendless, and so ill that she was in danger of dying. I could do nothing to help her while I was a prisoner myself."

Arabella thought she detected a tear glistening in the cor-ner of the earl's eye.

He sighed heavily. "It was a terrible dilemma for me. I finally capitulated to my father's demands, because it was the only way that I could save Nell and our unborn child."

Arabella's face was troubled. "But wasn't that unfair to the countess?"

"She did not want or love me any more than I did her," the earl said bitterly. "All she wanted was to be a countess and have a son who would be an earl. Even though I had eloped with another woman and refused for months after that to wed Henrietta, both she and her mother were determined to have the match."

Arabella wondered whether Henrietta had not reaped her just reward for her ambition, but still there was a note of dis-approval in her voice as she said to the earl, "So you married her and promptly went back to Nell."

He shook his head wearily. "No. I did not try at first to keep my part of the devil's bargain that we had made. I took care of Nell—and Damon when he was born—but I did not live with them for a year after I married Henrietta. Finally, though, I could take no more of her. The shrew wanted nei-ther a marriage nor a husband but a toady to grovel at her feet and perform her every whim as her father had for her mother. It was the most wretched year of my life. By that time I had inherited Willow Wood, and I came here with Nell, whom I still considered my true wife, and Damon."

That night after dinner the earl suggested a game of chess to his son, but Damon declined, saying he wanted to retire early.

"Brom and I are riding over to the west estate tomorrow," Damon explained. "There are several problems there that need my attention. I want to get a very early start. Even then I doubt that I shall be able to get back by tomorrow night."

When Arabella and Damon retired, he seemed to take special care to excite and please her. It was obvious to both of them that his endeavors were wildly successful.

Afterward, as she still lay in the protective warmth of his arms, she asked with disappointment in her voice, "Do you think you will be gone tomorrow night?"

It would be the first night that they had been separated since their wedding, and the thought of lying alone in this big tester bed without Damon was repugnant to Arabella.

"Will you miss me?" he asked lazily.

"Of course I will."

His arms released her. He raised himself on his elbow and stared down at her. His face was in shadow, but hers was illuminated by the light of the full moon that streamed through the windows. "Do you love me, Arabella?" he asked softly.

She lay silent, wondering why it mattered in the least to him when he did not love her.

"Do you?" he pressed.

The memory of the joy on his face as he had talked to Sally rose up in her mind. Jealousy stabbed at her, and she parried his question hotly. "Would you have my love, too? That was not included in the bargain with my father."

He stiffened and rolled away from her. He rose from the bed and went over to the windows, staring out into the moonlit night.

"What of you?" she cried, determined to know the identity of his "sweet, dearest love" that he had mistaken Arabella for in his sleep. "Who is the woman you love?"

He spun around in surprise to face her.

"I know there is somebody," Arabella told him. "Isn't there?"

"Yes."

Arabella wanted to burst into tears at his soft, almost reluctant answer, but she forced her voice to remain cold, almost disinterested. "Who is she?"

Damon came back to the bed and looked down at her as if he could not quite believe that she could ask him such a question. Somehow she managed to return his stare coolly. When at last he spoke, his voice was bitter. "That is my secret. We each came to this marriage with our secret loves. Except your stepmother revealed yours."

Arabella wanted to cry that she had never loved Estes. But if she did that, Damon would insist upon knowing the identity of the man she did love. She could not admit to him that he himself was the man. Not after he confirmed to her that he loved another woman.

"Why didn't you marry the woman you love, instead of me?" she demanded.

When he did not answer, Arabella pressed, "Does she not return your love?"

"No, she doesn't," Damon snapped, getting back into bed. "She cannot permit herself to love a bastard!"

The bitterness in his voice was so strong that Arabella almost blurted out, "Then she is a fool." But Arabella managed to hold her tongue.

Damon, keeping a careful distance between them in the bed, turned his back on her.

Perhaps he went to sleep. Arabella could not tell. She lay awake for hours, silent tears trickling down her face.

Chapter 21

The soft closing of a door nudged Arabella from an exhausted sleep. Opening her eyes, she saw her husband, dressed in riding coat and buckskin breeches, had emerged from his dressing room and was crossing toward the door to the hall. The pale hue of the light coming through the windows told her it was not long after dawn.

"Are you leaving already?" she asked sleepily.

The coldness in Damon's eyes as he looked at her shocked her instantly awake. She shivered as though she had just been drenched by a bucket of icy water. "Yes," he said curtly as his hand turned the handle of the door.

It was like a knife turning in Arabella's heart. He was not even going to kiss her good-bye.

"Damon, what is the matter?" she demanded as he stepped through the opened door.

His brown eyes seemed frozen as he turned them upon her. "I cannot forgive you for loving Estes. If it had been any other man, I could have. But not him!"

The door slammed and Damon was gone.

For a moment, Arabella lay stunned. What unspeakable thing had Estes done that had so turned Damon and his father, fair men both, against him.

Then tears trickled down her cheeks. What a mull she had made of it all. If only she had told Damon the truth that day he had been introduced to her at Lindley Park. Slowly her self-reproach gave way to a gathering determination that when Damon returned, she would make him listen to what her true feelings for him and for Estes were.

Even though Damon had admitted that he loved another woman, Arabella must swallow her pride and confess to him that he was the only man that she had ever loved. She should have done so long before now. Perhaps someday he could learn to love her as she loved him. But that could never happen until the specter of Estes was removed.

Arabella, her heart churning, spent the morning with her father-in-law, who remarked on her unusual quietness. "What has made you unhappy, Arabella?" he asked at last.

"I am anxious for Damon's return," she replied, telling him part of the truth.

In the afternoon the earl took a long nap.

Arabella, too restless to sit still, went outside to watch the work of Willow Wood's gardeners, who were refurbishing the formal flower beds at the front of the house under her direction.

As she started down the portico steps, she saw a rider galloping toward the house. She stopped, terrified that the man might be bringing word that Damon had met with an accident.

But when the rider wheeled to a stop before her, it was Lord Estes. Seeing Arabella on the portico steps, he dismounted and came toward her. His clothes were coated with dust, his boots were splattered with mud, and his horse was lathered.

It was hard to tell what shocked her more about Estes: his unexpected arrival or the change in him in recent weeks. He was even more carelessly dressed than he had been when she had seen him on her wedding day. His greasy hair did not appear to have been washed or his dirty, crumpled neck linen

changed since then. The blond stubble on his face had length-
ened into a thin, scraggly beard. There were deepening lines
of dissipation in his bloated face. He had abandoned the stays
that he had used to nip in his waist, and his body, which had
always tended toward the portly, now bulged at the fasten-
ings of his coat. But most disturbing by far to Arabella was
the wild, glittering look in his bloodshot eyes.

"Why are you here?" she demanded coldly. Damon would
be furious if he were to learn of Estes's visit. And what of her
father-in-law? She was thankful that his room was at the back
of the house with no view of the portico.

"Such a warm welcome for your former betrothed," Estes
sneered.

Arabella was desperate to be rid of him. "Please leave,"
she said firmly, "or I will be forced to summon my husband,
who will see that you do."

He laughed at her. "That won't wash. I am here because
I know that Damon is not. He is gone for the day."

"How did you know that?" Arabella was alarmed.

Estes laughed unpleasantly. "I have my spy. But never
mind that, I want to talk to you. I will not leave until I do so."
He gestured toward the gardeners, who were openly staring
at their mistress and the newcomer. "If you wish to avoid a
scene in front of those very interested workers over there, you
will listen to me. Besides, I have a proposition for you that
is so attractive you will not be able to refuse it."

His eyes shone with such a wild malevolence that she was
thoroughly frightened. As he stepped toward her, he reeked
of alcohol. He was drunk and mad in the bargain! It suddenly
struck Arabella that there was indeed a connection between
the two. Damon had been right. When Estes had been sober,
she had enjoyed his company, but when he had been drink-
ing, he seemed possessed by venomous hate. She had to find
out what he was scheming, but she must do so away from the
watching eyes and possibly acute hearing of the workers.

She led him to the house where the butler, Turpin, his face set in stern disapproval, barred the entrance, saying, "Mr. Howard has ordered that Lord Estes was never again to set foot in a house of his."

"You impertinent fool," Estes snapped. "You should have been sacked years ago."

"Stop it!" Arabella said, silencing Estes. Turning to Turpin, she said with quiet dignity, "I insist upon talking privately to Lord Estes in the withdrawing room for a few minutes."

The butler gave her a look that told her she had just made herself as unpopular with him as Lord Estes was.

"Is it your order, ma'am?" Turpin asked.

"Yes, it is," Arabella said calmly, hating Estes for putting her into this wretched position.

Turpin's lips were fixed in hard disapproval. "I tell you nothing good will come of inviting that young scoundrel in here. Mr. Howard will be very angry, and I shudder to think of the consequences should the earl learn of this."

Turpin was no doubt right, Arabella thought with an aching heart, but she had to learn what Estes was plotting.

In the privacy of the withdrawing room, Estes said bitterly to Arabella, "When I own this heap, I'll send that old fool packing quick enough."

"What do you mean? You will never own Willow Wood."

"Oh, but I shall! I am the rightful owner of all that my father once possessed, and you will help me recover what is rightfully mine." Estes's eyes glittered irrationally.

"What are you talking about?" Arabella demanded, even more frightened by his eyes than by his words.

"When your husband dies before an heir is born to you, you will inherit his estate."

"That is nonsense. There is no healthier man than Damon."

"That is why you and I must help him out of this world."

Arabella was unable to believe her ears. "You cannot be serious," she stammered. "You would *murder* your brother?"

"He is not my brother!" Estes exploded. "He is a bastard, nothing more! And you will help me regain what he has stolen from me. Poison will be the surest and quickest method to rid us of him. No one is in a better position to give it to him than you."

"You are mad, totally mad!" Arabella whispered in horror. "You should be locked up in Bedlam. Whatever made you think that I should agree to such an unspeakable scheme?"

"Because then I will marry you and you will share my title. Instead of being the wife of a lowly bastard, you will be the countess of Woodthorpe as well as possessor of the Howard fortune."

"You are worse than mad! You are diabolically evil!" Arabella walked to the door of the withdrawing room and flung it open. "Get out of here and don't ever set foot on Willow Wood again."

Estes stared at her as if she were the one who was mad. "You won't help me?"

"Of course I *won't* help you. You are the most disgusting human being I have ever met, if indeed you are even human! Now, get out."

He started for her with such rage in his eyes that she thought for a moment he meant to hit her. She seized a heavy bronze sculpture from a table and brandished it at him. "Come another step nearer me and I shall brain you!"

He checked himself and instead stumbled toward the door. There he turned back. "You fool, you will regret this. I shall have what is rightfully mine with or without your help!"

He slammed from the house. Arabella replaced the bronze

and grasped the edge of the table tightly to steady herself. Estes was mad!

And he would kill Damon.

Chapter 22

Damon and Brom did not return that night but sent word that they would be back in the early afternoon of the following day. The hours of their absence dragged by for Arabella. She was desperate to warn her husband about Estes, yet she dreaded having to face Damon's anger when he learned that his half brother had been to see her.

The next morning Arabella sought to bury her nervousness by arranging bouquets of flowers in the workroom that had been Nell's. Arabella was there when Brom suddenly burst in on her about eleven.

"You're back early!" she exclaimed. "Where is Damon?"

"He's gone up to see his father."

Arabella flinched. Of course, Damon would prefer seeing his father to seeing his wife, but still the knowledge rankled. She washed her hands and went slowly up the stairs to her bedroom. Damon was still with his father, and Arabella paced nervously as she waited for him.

When Damon entered the bedroom, Arabella's heart and tongue both floundered at the cold hardness that his face held for her.

"Damon," she stammered. "I must talk to you about Estes. He has been here."

"Yes, I know. Turpin told me." The iciness of Damon's tone told Arabella more plainly than a torrent of angry words how furious he was with her. "How could you invite Estes here?"

"I did not invite him!"

The triangular black eyebrows raised in disbelief. "He just happened to appear as soon as I left Willow Wood."

"I swear to you that I had nothing to do with his coming! You must believe me. I would never have invited him here!"

Her husband's eyes told Arabella that he did not believe her. "Then there is no point in discussing him further," Damon said coldly, turning toward the door to leave.

"Yes, there is," she cried, placing herself between him and the door. "Your life depends upon it. Estes means to kill you."

Damon regarded her impassively, without surprise.

"So?"

Arabella seized Damon's arms frantically. "Don't you understand what I am saying? Estes is mad. He is determined to kill you. For God's sake, listen to me, Damon. I tell you he will do it. You must believe me!"

"I believe you," Damon said casually, as though they were talking about nothing more significant than the weather. "But why would Estes tell you beforehand that he planned to kill me?"

"I told you: he is insane. He wanted me to help him."

Damon's face was emotionless. "What did he offer you in return—to make you his countess?"

"Yes."

"Will you help him?"

Arabella's eyes widened in horrified disbelief. "You are as mad as he is to ask me such a terrible question!"

"Am I?" Damon asked wearily. "Are you telling me that

you do not love Lord Estes quite enough to murder me to have him?''

''I never loved Estes, ever! By now I *loathe* him!''

''He says you adore him.''

''Yes, and he believes the sun, moon, and stars all revolve around him and that he can get away with your murder, too!''

Damon was unmoved. His eyes continued to regard her hostilely. ''But you loved him?''

''I never loved him. By the time he broke our betrothal, I was overjoyed to be rid of him.''

''But you wrote me that you loved him.''

''The man I wrote you of was not Estes.''

For the first time, Damon looked at her with a flicker of interest. ''Pray, then, who is this great love of yours?''

She hung her head. ''You will think me very foolish, I know, but I lost my heart to a stranger whom I met one midnight upon Hounslow Heath.''

Hope flared in Damon's dark eyes, then died as quickly as it had appeared, and was replaced by anger. ''Yes,'' he snapped. ''I do think you very foolish indeed. I will never believe such a Banbury tale as that. You disappoint me, Arabella. I did not think you a liar.''

''Why won't you believe me?'' Arabella cried in anguish as Damon stalked to the door and threw it open with a bang.

Turning back to her, he said with blazing eyes, ''Because if it were true, you would have told me long ago. There would have been no reason on earth for you to hide from your husband the fact that you loved him!''

The door slammed behind Damon with such force the windows rattled, and he was gone.

Arabella stared at the door, tears streaming from her eyes.

A moment later, she heard the bell that the earl used to summon servants ringing violently. He must have heard Damon's angry departure. She could not let the earl be upset.

Brushing her tears away, Arabella went slowly into her father-in-law's room and made her way to his bedside.

He was sitting up in his tester bed, his wasted body propped against several feather pillows. His eyes searched her face. "You and Damon had a fight." It was a statement, not a question.

She nodded.

The earl patted a spot beside him on the bed. "Sit here beside me, Arabella."

She settled herself on the bed as he had indicated and laid her hands in her lap.

"You will not find a better man than Damon," the earl told her softly. "He deserves your love and respect. I could not ask for a finer son, nor a woman for a better husband." Woodthorpe leaned back against the pillows, stared unseeingly into space for a few moments. Then he sighed sadly and said more to himself than to Arabella, "I have one good son and one bad. I have myself to blame for the bad."

She stared curiously at the frail head on the pillows. "What do you mean?"

"One of the requirements of my nefarious marriage agreement was that I would father a son on Henrietta. She wanted it, and I was determined to adhere scrupulously to that agreement. It took six miserable years for her to conceive Estes. What a mistake to have brought him into the world."

Woodthorpe shook his head disgustedly, as though in comment upon his own folly. "Once he was born, his mother, who detested me even more than I disliked her, refused to let me see him. I could have forced the issue, but I felt I should let her have the son that she had wanted so desperately. He grew up a stranger to me."

"How sad for you," Arabella murmured.

"Sad for me but disastrous for Estes." The earl's thin hands curled in frustration around the blanket that covered him. "And in the end, disastrous for us both."

"I don't understand," Arabella murmured.

"His mother spoiled him so badly that he grew into a weak, irresponsible man, lazy, cowardly, and unfit to manage the fortune he would inherit from me. I longed to instill some sense and steel in him. He came to me recently, asking me to settle his exorbitant gambling debts, and I saw my chance. In exchange, I insisted that he must live with me at Longbridge so that I could try to teach him as I had taught Damon."

"But he refused."

"Estes preferred a quicker solution to his debt problems," Woodthorpe said sardonically. "He thought that if I were dead, he would inherit everything."

A dozen fragments of seemingly unconnected conversation suddenly welded together in Arabella's mind into a seamless whole of meaning. She clapped her hands to her mouth in shock, then blurted, "That is why you have been so ill. Estes tried to kill you!"

The earl nodded. "He sneaked up and shot me in the back. Damon chanced upon us just as Estes fired, and deflected the shot slightly. It hit me in the gut instead of the heart, which is what Estes was aiming for. Still, it came very close to finishing me."

Arabella examined the terrible toll that Estes's perfidy had inflicted upon the earl—the wasted body, the pain-etched face, the hollow eyes—and wanted to weep for all that unnecessary suffering. No wonder Damon loathed his half brother and could not forgive Arabella for loving him.

Except that she did not love Estes, had never loved Estes. But how was she ever to convince Damon of that?

"Why have you kept what Estes did a secret?" she asked.

"Because I blame myself for the way he has turned out. I knew what his mother was like. I should never have let her have free reign with him. So my punishment of him has been more subtle. He will get none of the great fortune he so hungered for except Woodthorpe Hall.''

''And your title,'' Arabella reminded him.

''I wanted to deny him that, too, but Damon dissuaded me. He has no interest in it, and he did not want me to undergo the ordeal of the litigation that would be required.''

Arabella could not understand why a man who had married her only for social standing would have rejected the opportunity to be an earl. But at last she did understand why Damon had been so revolted by the thought that she loved Estes. Arabella sprang up from the earl's bed.

''I have to find Damon,'' she explained to her startled father-in-law. ''I have to make him believe that I love him more than anything in the world.''

She hurried to the window and snatched up the eyeglass. Damon often visited his mother's grave, and Arabella suspected he might be there now. Focusing the glass on the glade, she saw that her guess had been right. Damon was standing there, his head bowed.

As Arabella started to lower the glass, something else caught her eye: the glint of sun on metal in the ribbon of woods along the creek that ran very near the glade. She trained the glass on the spot.

Her heart somersaulted in terror. The metallic object was a gun in Estes's hands. He was creeping through the trees, stalking Damon.

Arabella stifled a scream and dropped the glass. Not wanting to alarm the earl, she said, ''I see Damon. I must go to him at once.'' She walked quickly from the room. Once its door was shut behind her, she ran as fast as she could down the steps, out the door, and toward the stable.

A groom was leading a frisky mare out for exercise. Arabella dashed up and snatched the reins from his hands. Throwing propriety to the winds, she grabbed up her skirts, thrust one foot in the stirrup and her other over the mare, flinging herself into the saddle in a cloud of petticoats.

She headed toward the glade, desperately urging the mare to a gallop. She prayed that she would reach Damon before Estes did.

Her eyes scanned the narrow woods for Estes. At last she saw him. He had made his way to a clump of the bushes not far from where Damon stood. Now, gun in hand, he rose up from behind them and took careful aim at Damon's back.

He's going to shoot Damon in the back just as he shot his father, Arabella thought, jabbing the mare roughly. The horse responded with a burst of speed that brought Arabella within hailing distance of Damon.

"Damon," she screamed at him. "Damon, look out behind you! Throw yourself to the ground!"

Hearing her, her husband turned to look in her direction. She saw Estes's finger tighten on the trigger.

"Throw yourself to the ground, Damon!" she screamed again, but her final words were drowned out by the thunderous crack of a shot.

Damon tumbled to the earth.

Feeling as though the bullet had lodged in her own heart, Arabella galloped up to the glade, jumped from the saddle in a whirl of petticoats and shapely leg, and ran to her husband.

He was lying on his back on the grass. To her relief, she saw that his eyes were open.

"Oh, thank God, you are alive," she cried as she dropped to her knees beside him. There was a hole torn through his left sleeve but very little blood on the cloth. "Are you all right?"

He grinned at her. "No, I am quite overcome by such a magnificent display of lovely legs."

"How can you joke at such a moment? I am speaking of your wound."

"Oh, the merest scratch, thanks to your warning. The ball

only grazed me. Had I not followed your advice and thrown myself to the ground, it probably would have caught me in the heart.''

"But this ball shall not miss your bastard's heart," Estes's cold voice told them.

Arabella turned and saw Estes standing above them, a pistol pointed at Damon's heart.

"No," Arabella cried, and threw herself over her husband so that her body covered his.

"Your wife's devotion is most touching," Estes said. "If she does not remove herself from you, I shall have to shoot her first."

"Arabella, for the love of God, get away from me," Damon hissed in her ear. "If you make a run for your horse now, you can escape with your life before he has time to reload."

"No, I won't," Arabella said stubbornly. "He will have to kill me before he can kill you!"

"You leave me no choice but to oblige you," Estes said.

"For God's sake, Arabella, save yourself!" her husband pleaded. "He will kill me whether you live or die."

Arabella clung all the more tenaciously to Damon. "No," she sobbed. "I do not want to live without you, Damon. I love you more than life itself."

"Don't be a fool," Damon cried. His arm encircled her. With a mighty effort he managed to roll over on it with her so that now she was beneath him.

Arabella was now on her back upon the ground with her body protected by Damon's, which was prone across hers. Arabella saw Estes raise his pistol and point it at Damon's back.

"No, Estes," Arabella cried, her eyes blazing up at him. "You will accomplish nothing by killing Damon except your own destruction."

Estes hesitated.

His eyes were not bloodshot, and he did not appear drunk.

If he was sober, perhaps she could reason with him. She had to try. Her tongue was the only weapon she had to save Damon.

"Killing Damon will not gain you his fortune," she said. She felt her husband's hand stealing surreptitiously into the pocket of his coat as she held Estes's attention. "It is lost to you forever."

"No! When he is dead, you will marry me," Estes insisted, but there was uncertainty in his eyes.

"If you harm Damon, I will not rest until I see you hanged on Tyburn Hill!" Arabella cried.

Her vehemence startled Estes, and he lowered his pistol slightly.

"Don't be a fool, Estes," she pleaded. "Shooting Damon will not win you the fortune that you lost. All it will bring you is certain public punishment and shame. You will not escape it as you did last time. I promise you that!"

Damon rolled half off Arabella, so that his back was no longer to Estes. His right hand was still in his pocket.

"She is right, Estes," Damon said calmly. "You have nothing to gain and everything to lose. Our father will not let you escape so easily this time. Drop your gun, Estes, and this incident will remain private between us."

The eyes of the half brothers locked. Although Damon was helpless upon the ground, his gaze was cool and fearless. It was Estes, holding a wavering pistol, who was frightened. Grudging admiration crept into his eyes for Damon.

"Drop the gun, Estes," Damon repeated quietly.

"No!" Estes gasped. "You will kill me if I do."

"I swear to you, Estes, that if you drop the gun, I will not harm you in any way."

The hand holding the pistol was shaking now, and Estes muttered, "God, I need a drink! I should never have come here without getting foxed first."

"Courage out of a bottle is no courage at all," Damon said.

"I am not a coward!" Estes flared.

"Prove it to me by dropping your gun," Damon said. "That takes real courage, Estes."

Still Estes held the gun pointed at Damon.

CHAPTER 23

Arabella could see reflected in Estes's eyes the emotions warring within him. She unconsciously held her breath. Damon's life depended upon the outcome of that interior battle.

Finally, reluctantly, Estes let the pistol fall to the earth.

Arabella drew a long gasp of air into her bursting lungs. "Thank God," she murmured.

Damon scrambled to his feet. "That was a wise as well as courageous decision, Estes. It saved your life." Damon removed his right hand from his pocket and displayed a small pistol. "This was aimed at you. If you had tightened your finger on that trigger, I would have shot you."

The color drained from Estes's face and he looked as though his knees would buckle. Damon placed a firm, supporting hand on his half brother's arm. Estes flinched and quavered, "You promised you wouldn't hurt me."

"Nor will I." Damon's hand dropped away from Estes. "If I had wanted to do that, I would have shot you. You gave me ample excuse."

Estes, who was nearly a foot shorter than Damon, stared up at his giant of a half brother with mingled uncertainty and fear. "What will you do to me?"

"Nothing," Damon replied. "I told you that if you

dropped the gun, this incident would remain private between us. You did, and it will. You're free to go provided that you leave Kent at once.''

Clearly fearing that Damon would have a change of heart, Estes turned and fled as fast as his stubby legs could carry his portly body.

As Arabella watched him run toward the horse that he had hidden in the ribbon of woods along the creek, she whispered to Damon, ''You can't let him go. He may come back and kill you.''

''I doubt it,'' Damon said, returning the little pistol to his pocket. ''He has to flee England by the end of the week if he is to escape debtors' prison. I shall help him with a one–way passage abroad.''

''To where? France?''

''I prefer a trifle more distance between us,'' Damon said dryly. ''My choice would be China, but I suppose I shall have to settle for India.'' He gestured impatiently. ''Enough, however, of Estes. I have something of infinitely greater importance to attend to.''

Damon's words conjured in Arabella's mind mountains of ledgers and documents that would again claim his attention for the remainder of the day. Disappointment wrenched her heart, and she asked testily, ''What is of such importance?''

''A wife who has at last admitted she loves me.'' Damon wrapped Arabella in his arms, a teasing grin playing on his face. ''You cannot know how much I have longed for you to assure me that you loved me. But in my wildest dreams I never imagined that you would do so in such an emphatic and convincing manner, my dearest love.''

''You love me?'' she asked incredulously, her azure eyes alight with hope.

''Why else would I have married you?''

The glow died in her eyes. ''For social position. You told me so that day at Lindley Park.''

"Peagoose," he said lovingly, tightening his arms about her. "I was so irritated that you could think such a thing that I was being sarcastic. I don't give a damn about social position."

Arabella stared up at him in confusion, wondering if the strain of the day had addled him. "But you insisted on being married in London in that grand ceremony with all the ton present."

His dark eyes gleamed. "I assure you that I had an even livelier dread of our elaborate wedding than you did of our wedding night."

"Then why did you insist upon it?"

"For you, my love. To assure your continued acceptance in society. As I wrote your aunt, being married with all that pomp and circumstance under her aegis would do that." Damon's eyes were no longer shuttered, and Arabella felt as though she were being wrapped in soft brown velvet. "You had told me that night we met that you could not bear to be ostracized as my mother was."

"But that was before I discovered what it was to love as much as I loved you!" Arabella protested. "After that, I no longer cared. I was proud to be your wife."

"Nevertheless, I loved you too much to chance making you a pariah."

His mouth settled over hers in a long, passionate kiss that left no doubt in either's mind of the depth of their feelings for each other.

When he lifted his lips from hers, his face was puzzled. "But if you fell in love with me that night we met, why the devil would you not tell me so?"

"Mostly I was ashamed to admit how much I loved you when you did not return my love," Arabella confessed. "And I feared that you would think me a silly green girl to have lost my heart to a stranger on our first meeting."

"Why would I think that when I, too, lost my heart on

Hounslow Heath to a courageous, impetuous innocent in buckskin breeches, glorious azure eyes, delightful dimples, and a forthrightness that was as refreshing as it was rare?''

"You did?" she exclaimed in disbelief.

"I did," he replied firmly, his fingertips gently stroking her face.

"Then why did you not kiss me again in the stable before you left that night?"

"I knew that if I had tasted your lips again, I would never be able to forget you, and I was determined to do so. You had told me most emphatically that you would never consider an ineligible suitor, and I could not have been more ineligible.'' Damon's face hardened at the memory. "But by the time we met again, I knew that my resolve was futile. You were indelibly inscribed in my heart. And you seemed so happy to see me that day outside Getz's that I began to hope that perhaps I could win your heart."

"How did you expect to do so when you never came near me?'' Arabella demanded indignantly. "You might at least have called on me."

Damon gave a shout of laughter. "My dearest Arabella, what reception would I have gotten had I informed Lady Vaughn that I wished to court you?''

Arabella blushed at what that scene would have been like. She ran her fingers along the strong, broad face that she loved so much, and suddenly her eyes sparkled teasingly. "But if you had truly loved me, you would have found a way to see me.''

"I did, but you ruined it! I persuaded poor Sally Cromwell that she should get you to visit her without your stepmother.''

"You were Sally's surprise that day," Arabella cried.

He laughed. "Yes, but it was Sally and I who got the surprise. You cannot imagine our consternation when Lady Vaughn drove up without you. I was forced to sneak out a side door like a clandestine lover to avoid meeting your stepmother.''

Arabella said raggedly, ''Lady Vaughn saw you, though. She was certain that you were Sally's lover.''

Arabella's tone banished the laughter from Damon's eyes. ''Don't tell me that you thought so, too!'' His voice echoed his startled disbelief.

''I . . . I wondered.''

Damon looked so shattered that Arabella felt miserable for having ever entertained such a suspicion. She tried to explain. ''I saw Sally talking to you the day after our return, and you looked so happy.''

''I was. She knew how concerned I was that marriage to me would make you an outcast, too. She had come to reassure me that I need not worry.'' Damon frowned indignantly at his wife. ''I swear there has never been anything between Sally and me.''

Arabella hugged him to her in silent assurance that she believed him.

Damon's anger gave way to amusement, and a wicked grin played on his lips. ''But as I recall, you did invite—indeed, urge—me to take a mistress.''

Arabella's arms fell away from Damon. ''Would you?'' she asked in a stricken voice.

He caressed her lovingly. ''Arabella, I told you once that I demanded fidelity of my wife. Do you think I would demand any less of myself?''

''But all those stories.''

He lowered his face very close to hers. His breath was warm and seductive upon her cheek. ''But no woman that I wanted to shackle myself to until I met you.''

Arabella's azure eyes mirrored her confusion. ''But if you loved me, Damon, why did you object so strenuously to marrying me when Papa proposed it? That was what convinced me that you could not possibly love me.''

"My objections were not because I did not love but because I loved you too much. I wanted to woo and win your heart, not have you told that you must marry me to save your father."

"But why did you never tell me that you loved me?"

"I wanted to hear first that you loved me. All of my life, I have been rejected because of my birth." The pain in Damon's voice was palpable. "Although your eyes and your body bespoke love, your tongue was mute. When you would not confess that you loved me, I thought it because you were ashamed to admit it even to yourself."

Damon's bitter words flashed through Arabella's mind: *"She cannot bring herself to love a bastard."*

"So I was your secret love, just as you were mine," Arabella breathed, clinging fiercely to Damon as though she were trying to squeeze from him any lingering doubt he might have about her love.

His embrace became as crushing as hers. His mouth claimed hers in a hungry, passionate kiss that was by turns possessive and wondering, demanding and tender.

When at last it ended, a shaken and breathless Arabella asked reproachfully, "How could you have doubted that I loved you?"

"How indeed!" Damon's eyes gleamed. "First there was your letter to me full of glowing compliments like 'ugly brute' and 'presumptuous baseborn boor.' Then there was your reassuring insistence that you loved another man and that nothing could be more repugnant to you than intimacy with me."

"I did not know who you were when I wrote that."

"But I was absolutely certain when I received it that you had to know! I was never so infuriated in my life. Then you would not confess the identity of your mysterious love. But your stepmother and Estes both assured me that he was the lucky man, and you did not deny it. No, my darling, you gave me no reason at all to doubt your love, did you?"

"I can see why you could have become a tiny bit concerned," she admitted. Then her eyes sparkled impishly. "But henceforth I shall tell you I adore you so often that you will become heartily sick of hearing it."

He grinned as his lips slowly descended to reclaim hers. "That, my love, is not possible."

27 million Americans can't read a bedtime story to a child.

It's because 27 million adults in this country simply can't read.

Functional illiteracy has reached one out of five Americans. It robs them of even the simplest of human pleasures, like reading a fairy tale to a child.

You can change all this by joining the fight against illiteracy.

Call the Coalition for Literacy at toll-free **1-800-228-8813** and volunteer.

**Volunteer
Against Illiteracy.
The only degree you need
is a degree of caring.**

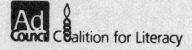

**Ad
Council** Coalition for Literacy

LV-3